The Tragedy of
ROCKY
The Very PICTURE of HORROR

by
Nicholas Dollak

(With illustrations by the author.)

The Tragedy of
ROCKY
The Very PICTURE of HORROR

Persons Represented.

Doctor **Faustus Frank N. Furter**, *Philosopher, Lord of the Castle and a Transvestite*
Duke **Rocky Horror**, *an Homunculus, Creation of* Dr. Frank N. Furter.
Riff-Raff, *a Jack-of-all-Trades.*
Magenta, *a Domestic.*
Mistress **Columbia**, *Mistress to* Dr. Frank N. Furter.
Lady **Janet Weiss**, *a Gentlewoman, betrothed of* Brad Majors.
Lord **Brad Majors**, *a Gentleman.*
Doctor **Everett the Scot**, *a Philosopher, Opposite to* Dr. Frank N. Furter, *and Uncle to* Edward Cutlet.
Edward Cutlet, *a former Page-boy to* Frank N. Furter.
The Bard

Sir **Ralph Hapschatt**, *a Gentleman.*
Lady **Beatrice Munroe**, *a Gentlewoman.*

Groundlings, Gentlemen *and* **Gentlewomen** *in the Audience.*

Wedding attendants, Transylvanians, Singers, a Choir &c.

And Special Guest Appearance by **Greasy Joan**.

Scene, - *In the* **Apartments** *of a Gentleman and Gentlewoman;* *then a* **Churchyard** *after a Wedding in* **Denton, Ohio** ; *afterwards on a* **Road** ; *then at the* **Castle** *of Dr. Frank N. Furter.*

1 **Induction:** Shakespeare's word for what we would today call an Introduction

2 **opposing:** approaching from opposite directions

3 **Forsooth!:** Indeed! An exclamation of consternation.

4 **raiment:** clothing

5 **unseemly:** inappropriate

6 **masque:** a play performed in masks or interesting costumes

7 **mark:** understand

INDUCTION.

An Apartment in town.
Enter a GENTLEMAN and GENTLEWOMAN, opposing.

GENTLEWOMAN
Forsooth! Are we not setting out to the theatre?
Thy raiment is most unseemly.

GENTLEMAN
Dear lady, be of good humor and kind disposition.
These cloths are but the semblance of what we shall see
upon the stage tonight.

GENTLEWOMAN
Thou'rt not an actor. My father married me to a
respectable man. Hast thou deceiv'd him?

GENTLEMAN
Nay! This costume is but custom,
if thou catch'st my meaning.
For the play we are to attend is like Carnival.
A masque not merely for players, but for
all present. An experience shared.

GENTLEWOMAN
I hear thy words, but mark not their meaning.
I suspect some game's afoot.

8 **scurrilous:** amusing

9 **queer:** Not what you think. In Shakespeare's day, and up until the 1960s, it meant "strange".

10 **Pray, mark my words:** Please, listen up.

11 **Fie!:** Nonsense!

GENTLEMAN
Verily! A most scurrilous
and right honorable game.
But thou hast not attired thyself fittingly.

GENTLEWOMAN
Those rags, strange and queer,
that were in my chambers?

GENTLEMAN
Aye! Those... rags.

GENTLEWOMAN
I'll not sally forth in those. I'll not present
my ankles and bosom in a public place.

GENTLEMAN
Pray, mark my words.
You will seem most overdressed,
you shall see.

GENTLEWOMAN
Fie! What manner of play is this?

GENTLEMAN
The best in this kind are but shadows,
and the worst are no worse,
if imagination amend them.

GENTLEWOMAN
Oh. *That* manner of play.

12 **enjoin:** join

13 <u>**jibes and fleers:**</u> snide remarks; taunts

14 *ex tempore*: Latin for ad lib, which is an abbreviation of *ad libitum*, which is Latin for *ex tempore*...

15 **groundlings:** poorer folk, who paid less for tickets and enjoyed the play while standing the whole time. Also called "penny-stinkers" after their cost-of-admission and to imply that they smelled worse than the well-heeled.

16 **nigh:** near

17 **outstrips:** outdoes

18 **lechery:** gaudiness

19 **maidenhead:** virginity

GENTLEMAN
Fair lady! Do but enjoin me this e'en,
and you shall see a merriment
made much the merrier by our own jibes and fleers.
For example, when the Singer do appear,
none will scorn you if you were to bid him sing.

GENTLEWOMAN
Truly?

GENTLEMAN
Aye, verily so, and that be but the start.
You may do it all *ex tempore*, as you see fit,
and speak it all full-throat,
that the nobles and the groundlings
alike can hear your words,
and praise thee for thy witty note.

GENTLEWOMAN
The time is nigh. We must away
if we are to find fitting seats.
I pray that none mock thee for thy garb.

GENTLEMAN
None shall, for there will be many
whose attire far outstrips mine for lechery.
One precaution must you take, my lady:
When one enquires after your maidenhead –

GENTLEWOMAN
Nay!

20 **'Tis tricksy.:** He means, it is difficult to explain. This is also a
play on words, as the opening song was originally sung (in the
premiere stage presentation of *The Rocky Horror Show*) by one
Trixie, who was a young lady who sold ice-cream at the theater's
concession stand.

21 **Curtain:** The theaters where Shakespeare's plays premiered
generally did not have curtains, so such a cue does not appear in
the plays that make up his canon. This is a liberty I have taken to
facilitate the staging of this work. I suppose it could be performed
without a curtain; but bear in mind that the lighting effects that
usually stand in for a curtain these days were completely non-
existent. The roof opened to the sky, and if darkness fell, torches
would be lit.

GENTLEMAN
Precisely. Thou did'st lose it long ago.
Elsewise, they will seat you among the groundlings.

GENTLEWOMAN
O what manner of play be this?

GENTLEMAN
'Tis tricksy. But soft – Here are our seats.
Come, madam wife, sit by my side,
and let the world slip.

> *Curtain falls as GENTLEMAN and*
> *GENTLEWOMAN leave the Stage and take*
> *their Seats.*

22 **These foursquare planks:** This stage

23 **samite:** a heavy silk fabric, often woven with gold or silver thread, used to make clothing in the Middle Ages

PROLOGUE.

Enter a SINGER, painted full of lips.

GENTLEWOMAN
Pray, sing to us, O Lips!

SINGER [*Sings.*]
Good Gentles, mark the traffic of our stage
whereof I lip-sing, two plays for the price of one.
Brief, pithy chronicles of future age,
and visions, past the wit of Man of which to say,
that do appear to us like fever'd dreams.
These foursquare planks do many worlds portray.
How Michael of the House of Rennie ail'd
and stillness thro' the Earth that day prevail'd,
yet tho' he lay, did tell us where we stand.

GENTLEMAN
On our feet, methinks!

SINGER
Our Saviour, all in silver'd samite clad,

GROUNDLING
Flash!!! A-ahhhh!

SINGER
Was there, as was Sir Claudio –
Claudio who discharg'd his part unseen.

24 **discharg'd:** carried out

25 **Philosophy and Fable:** In Shakespeare's day, the study of the natural world was part of the broader field of learning called "philosophy". Nowadays, the study of the natural world is Science, and Philosophy is primarily concerned with ethics and sociology. Fable, of course, is the telling of stories, generally with a moral.

26 **dross:** stuff, inanimate material

27 **anon:** soon, later on

28 ***Tempest* adaptation:** The classic 1956 science-fiction film *Forbidden Planet* is based on Shakespeare's final play *The Tempest*.

29 **Fa la la la la...:** nonsense syllables, quite common in English folk songs. Others are "hey, nonny-nonny", "derry-dong, derry-dong", "heigh-ho, the merry-o". Sort of like "hey, hey, hey", "yeah", or "baby" in today's pop songs.

GROUNDLING
Huh. He said "discharged"!

GENTLEMAN
T'was most dishonorable a discharge,
if e'er I saw one!

SINGER
A tragic tale did play, of Lady Wray,
favor'd beauty of bold King Kong, and how,
their lovers' stars were cross'd, love won and lost,
and thus was mighty monarch laid full low.

GROUNDLING
Huh. He said "laid"!

SINGER
Then from the Dome of Heaven fell –
I know not what; I cannot tell...
It did speak to us its message thus:
Philosophy and Fable, both alike in virtue,
together grant a physician means
to create from dross a life anew!
Or bring the full tumult of war
fought not by men, but by machines.
Brad and Janet, too, were there,

GROUNDLING
Were queer!

SINGER
whom thou wilt see anon.
And Anne Francis fair my Miranda were
in Tempest *adaptation.*
Fa la la la la...

30 **runes:** the written letters of the ancient Druids, also applied to words or whole sentences. In *The Rocky Horror Picture Show*, this is a reference to the 1957 film *Curse of the Demon*, adapted from M.R. James' 1911 short story "Casting the Runes", sometimes reprinted as "Passing the Runes".

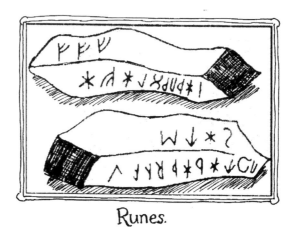

Runes.

31 **I would fain also go:** I'd like to go, too

At the nighttime revels I tell thee of,
two plays for the price of one.

Carrol the Lionhearted, of mighty mettle,
did smite Tarantula's long-legged stalks.
And Jeanette of Scotland, in fine fettle,
did vanquish a forest that walks.
Runes were as Greek to Lord Dana Andrews,
yet he marshaled his skills and did them pass.
Disasters in the Sun do seal our doom,
said friend George to his wife...

GROUNDLING
What a gas!

in a manner not unlike...
Philosophy and Fable, both alike in virtue,
together grant a physician means
to create from dross a life anew!
Or bring the full tumult of war
fought not by men, but by machines.
Brad and Janet, too, were there,
whom thou wilt see anon.
And Anne Francis fair my Miranda were
in Tempest *adaptation.*
Fa la la la la...
At the nighttime revels I tell thee of,
two plays for the price of one.
I would fain also go,
Hey, nonny-nonny go ho...
to the nighttime revels I tell thee of.
Where groundlings stand, there stand I,

32 **Pox on...:** Disease upon... Basically, "Screw them!"

33 **Exit:** He or she leaves

GENTLEMAN
Pox on the groundlings!

GROUNDLING
Yeah! Pox on the groundhogs!

With a hie-diddy, hie-diddy, hie-diddy, hie...
at the nighttime revels I tell thee of.

Exit SINGER.

34 **severally:** one at a time, or in small groups

35 **What, ho!:** exclamation of surprise, or to look alert

36 **sirrah:** a sarcastic form of "sir", meant disrespectfully

37 **plumb-bob:** a tool for gauging straight lines and perpendicularity

A Plumb-Bob.

38 **I mark thee not:** literally, I disregard what you say. Here, it is employed as a pun.

ACT I.

SCENE 1. – Denton. *Outside a Church.*
Enter WEDDING GUESTS severally,
among them BRAD and JANET.

FIRST GUEST
What, ho! They come!

GROUNDLING
Huh! He said "ho" and "come"!

SECOND GUEST
Were I a painter, then would I study these faces,
as though I would draw a portrait.

FIRST GUEST
You jest, sirrah! Thou canst not draw an even stroke
even though plumb-bob and compass be at hand.

SECOND GUEST
I can so draw, although I mark thee not.
I would assemble them all in array –
parents, grandparents, children in front...
Verily, all the close family.

Enter RALPH and BEATRICE.

GUEST
Good newlyweds, thou art well-met!
Blessings upon your house.

39 **wherefore:** Why

40 **boon companions:** close friends

41 **I had feigned:** I would have faked

42 **a tucket of trumpets:** A triumphant trumpet fanfare

GENTLEMAN
Wherefore have we two ears?

ALL
Hear, hear!

RALPH
Brad, old friend! Your presence here adds radiance
to this happy day.

GROUNDLING
I smell a fight!

They fight. Neither wins.

GENTLEMAN
Call ye that a fight?

RALPH
To think that tonight I go to my bed a married man.

BRAD
Of that, Sir Ralph, there is no doubt.
You and Lady Beatrice had been as boon companions
since childhood, when your tutor gave you lessons.

RALPH
In truth, were Betty not there,
I had feigned illness many a time, and played truant.

A tucket of trumpets.

43 **maidens:** Several jokes are at play here. While "maiden" may be regarded as an archaic term for "young lady", it strictly means "virgin" – as all well-bred young ladies were expected to be until they were wed. The Gentleman's cat-call could imply that they aren't all virgins. However, in Shakespeare's day, all the actors were men, even if they were playing female roles; therefore, virgins or not, they were none of them maidens.

44 **nuptials:** wedding, marriage

45 **vouchsafed:** assured

46 **Hymen:** Again, not what you think. Hymen was the Greek goddess of newlyweds. (And that, boys and girls, is why the hymen is so named.)

GUEST
Lady Beatrice will now cast the bouquet!
Maidens, come hither.
Who catches it, the next bride shall be!

BEATRICE
Maidens, at ready!

GENTLEMAN
He said "maidens"! You can't fool us!

LADY BEATRICE casts the bouquet. JANET catches it.

JANET
In truth, 'tis mine!

GUEST
Nay, 'tis mine!

JANET and several WOMEN fight. JANET wins.

JANET
Be just and fear not! My nuptials are vouchsafed.

RALPH
Methinks Hymen may cast a favorable eye
'pon you anon, sirrah.

BRAD
Perhaps. Dame Fortune bites her tongue
on matters of the heart.

RALPH
My carriage draws near. Brad, I bid thee adieu.
Come, Beatrice, my fair bride; let us away.

47 **Exeunt:** They exit

48 **now she is the property...:** Such was the role of women at the time, unfortunately.

Exeunt RALPH and BEATRICE.
Exeunt GUESTS severally.

JANET
O Brad, a more wond'rous wedding I had never seen!
All radiant was Beatrice, resplendent in her finery,
past all belief. But an hour ago she was a maid;
now she is the property of Sir Ralph.

BRAD
Aye, Janet. I drink to Ralph's good fortune.

JANET
Aye.

GUEST
Always do I weep at nuptials.

GENTLEMAN
And laugh at funerals!

BRAD
Beatrice will tend to her lord's needs now,
keeping him fatly fed.

JANET
Aye.

BRAD
She will all but vanish from public life,
while her lord the king's own favor enjoys.

JANET
Aye.

49 **forbear your exeunt:** don't leave just yet

50 **ban:** to swear or lay blame on something

Lord
Brad Majors.

Lady
Janet Weiss.

BRAD
Janet, attend.

JANET
Yes, Brad?

BRAD
Musicians! Pray, forbear your exeunt.
I have a song to sing, O.

JANET
Sing me your song, O.

GENTLEWOMAN
Spare us your song, O!

BRAD
Fair Janet, I stand amazèd at your display
of skill in seizing the bridal bouquet,
and how you did beat the other maidens...

GROUNDLING
Beat 'em to a pulp!

GENTLEWOMAN
Nor were they all maidens!

BRAD
... away.
[*Sings.*]
    Dover's channel is wide, yet I swam it, Janet.
    My castle has walls hewn from granite, Janet.
    Forgive me if I must curse and ban-it, Janet.
    I've but one oath to swear and that's
    'Zounds! Janet, I speak thee fair.

51 **shanks:** legs. Perhaps a reference to King Edward I of England (1239-1307), also known as Edward Longshanks for his long legs. He was a notoriously harsh ruler as concerns Scotland, and it is likely that Lord Brad still harbors much ill-will toward him.

52 **a non-rhyming planet:** Irrational belief in astrology's validity was at least as rife in Shakespeare's day as it is today.

53 **Gadzooks! 'Zounds!:** mild oaths

Gadzooks = "God's hooks" – the nails used to nail Christ to the cross

'Zounds = "God's wounds" – the wounds inflicted by same nails

54 **my whole troth:** all my loyalty; my promise

55 **naughty:** bearing no fruit; barren

56 **dowry:** money or other property given by the bride's family to her husband. Should the marriage fail, the dowry must be returned as well as the bride. This is still customary in several cultures today.

57 **Ophelia:** the girlfriend of Hamlet in Shakespeare's play of that name, who loses her sanity.

58 **O spite! O Hell!:** So much swearing... tsk, tsk...

The shanks were long but I span it, Janet.
I'd sing a better song but I cannot, Janet.
'Twas born 'neath a non-rhyming planet, Janet.
My love drives me mad – Gadzooks!
'Zounds! Janet, I speak thee fair.

GROUNDLING
Dammit, Janet, you reek down there!

BRAD
Here's my ring to prove I pledge my whole troth.
Love's green branches three ways do grow:
Fruitful, or naughty, or... maybe both.
O, J-A-N-E-T, my love to show.

JANET [*Sings.*]
Thy ring outshines Betty's; I'm so glad, O Brad.
Our troth thus seal'd, joy's to be had, O Brad!
My kin a dowry will so add, O Brad.
Like Ophelia, I've gone mad, O Brad, of love for thee.
O Brad...

BRAD
O spite!

JANET
I'm mad...

BRAD
O Hell, Janet!

JANET
... for thee...

The Bard.

BRAD
> *Then love have we!*

BOTH
> *One thing's yet to done be!*

BRAD
> *We must visit the man who began it, Janet,*
> *The philosopher Scot, Doctor Everett, Janet,*
> *Who tutored us both the whole gamut, Janet.*
> *I've but one oath to swear and that's*
> *'Zounds! Janet, I speak thee fair.*
> *'Zounds, Janet...*

> > > GENTLEMAN and GROUNDLING
> > > *Dammit, Janet, you reek down there!*

JANET
> *O Brad, I'm mad...*

BRAD
> *'Zounds, Janet...*

BOTH
> *I love thee...*

> > *Exeunt BRAD, JANET and MUSICIANS.*
> > *Enter THE BARD.*

> > > GENTLEMAN
> > > This man hath no neck!

THE BARD
If it pleaseth you –

60 **whither:** where is...?

61 **Marry:** Truthfully

62 **ruff:** frilly article of clothing worn over the collar

A Ruff.

63 **lay on:** continue

64 **vellum parchment:** high-quality paper made of sheepskin

65 **caution to the circumspect:** a word to the wise

66 **betroth'd:** betrothed, or one to whom one is engaged.

67 **even-tide:** evening

GROUNDLING
Where's yer neck?

THE BARD
Ahem. If it do please you –

GENTLEWOMAN
Pray, whither thy neck?

THE BARD
Marry, my lady, 'tis 'neath my ruff.

GENTLEMAN
And a rough neck it is. Do lay on, O Bard.

THE BARD
I shall relate to you a tale,
a tale of a journey most strange,
scribbl'd here on vellum parchment,
that it may serve as caution
to the circumspect.

GROUNDLING
Aw, is he gonna *read* to us or something?!?

THE BARD
'Twas in Denton town our tale begins.
Two of the youthful sort, of ordinary health,
Lord Brad Majors and Janet Weiss, now his betroth'd,
did set out that even-tide for the home
of one Doctor Everett, the Scot,
once their tutor, now their friend.

68 **dalliances:** messings-around, usually of a sexual nature. There are frequent mentions of dalliance in the script, of course.

69 **pendulous with portent of storm:** heavy, and threatening to rain

GENTLEMAN
Pray, sir, in troth,
Are you partial to dalliances with sheep?

GENTLEWOMAN
O forsooth!

THE BARD
'Tis true –

GENTLEMAN
Verily, I knew it to be true!

THE BARD
'Tis true that dark clouds,
pendulous with portent of storm,
did gather before them as their carriage did speed.

GROUNDLING
Hey, is it also true that, y'know... Um, your Mom? Uh...

THE BARD
Furthermore, 'tis true that a wheel
on that same carriage a split pin did have.
But being of the youthful sort, and of ordinary health,
they took them no heed of precaution,
nor the storm clouds fear'd.
No downpour of rain, no peals of thunder
nor fiery forks that split the sky ablaze,
did they dread, such was their resolve
to make of the evening such delights as they will'd.
An evening that would, ere long,
draw into night most wearying.

Exit THE BARD.

70 **this sceptered isle:**
This royal throne of kings, *this sceptered isle*,
This earth of majesty, this seat of Mars,
This other Eden, demi-paradise,
This fortress built by Nature for herself
Against infection and the hand of war,
This happy breed of men, this little world,
This precious stone set in the silver sea,
Which serves it in the office of a wall
Or as a moat defensive to a house,
Against the envy of less happier lands, -
This blessed plot, this earth, this realm, this England.

- Shakespeare, *King Richard II*, Act 2, scene 1

71 **bespate:** spattered with mud

SCENE 2. – Denton. *A Forest at Night. Rain and Thunder.*

Enter BRAD and JANET.
BRAD carries a Wheel.

GENTLEMAN
O Brad, tell us sad tales on the deaths of kings!

BRAD
And though he did slay five Richmonds 'pon the field,
Richmond could he not find. His horse slain,
his men fled, he cried, "A horse!
My kingdom for a horse!"
though he were loathe to quit.
Aye, Richard was a tricksy Dick,
but not a quitter he.

GROUNDLING
Tricky Dickie!

JANET
Yea; this sceptered isle doth need a king full-time,
and lords and vassals besides.
This rain soaks me to the quick,
my clothes bespate.
Wherefore did thy carriage this opportunity take
to throw a wheel?

BRAD
Aye. Mine own lands for a horse,
and some dry clothes. What, ho!

72 **Prithee:** Please! (a contraction of "I pray thee")

73 **tarry:** pause, hang around

74 **contagion:** sickness

GROUNDLING
Huh! He said "ho" again!

BRAD
Come some riders. Prithee, halt!

Enter TRANSYLVANIANS, moving at Speed.

JANET
O muddied! Why gallop they so,
in such weather as this?
That they not tarry a bit to help us
is cruel enough. Should one slip
and brain himself upon a stone...

BRAD
Aye, Janet, they do but hold life as cheap.

GENTLEMAN
They do hold their manhoods cheap as well!

JANET
These paths do wind in ways mysterious.
Are we yet bound for Doctor Everett's mansion?

BRAD
The road doth fork and fork again.
We are set upon the wrong path.

He sets down the Wheel and kicks it.

Though I dealt this wheel a manly kick,
yet it remains broken – O wicked wheel!
and we remain lost. And this rain
will bring contagion 'pon us ere long.
I glimpsed a castle not far off; perhaps

75 **doth become:** is appropriate behavior for

76 **make free with you:** take advantage of you

there we can find a warm hearth and a dry bed.

JANET
I go with you, but let you sleep at a distance.
Such separation doth become a bachelor and a maid.

                                    GROUNDLING
                        Prude! Yo, Brad! I think her legs
                            are shackled at the knee!

BRAD
Janet, one mattress will serve us both if need be.

JANET
You speak in jest, my lord, and some may think me prude.
But I reconsider; one mattress may be yet prudent,
if the castle be the home of a beautiful woman,
who means to make free with you.

BRAD
And free she may be to do so!

JANET
O wicked! You do mock me, sir.
I, who have no recourse but to –
But what this? A sign.

                                    GENTLEMAN
                        Pray, what say it? What say it?

JANET
At... risk... of... thine... own... life...

GENTLEWOMAN
Haste, Janet! Make not a banquet
of but the merest mouthful of words!

JANET
... and... thine... own... soul...
I... do... beseech... thee...
forebear... to... enter... unto... here.

GROUNDLING
Was I asleep? Did she finish reading the sign yet?

JANET
... and a point of exclamation it doth make.

GENTLEMAN
And thus is she now finishèd.

JANET
Nay; for I feel a song coming.

GROUNDLING
She feels it coming! And no thanks to Brad!

JANET
[*Sings.*]
 In velvet darkness of the night most black
 a beacon teaches torches burn bright,
 As constant as the Northern Star, and back;
 No matter who thou art, it giveth light.

77 **espy:** spy, see

78 **Frankish:** constructed in the style of the Franks, an assortment of Germanic peoples who inhabited Roman Gaul and later controlled much of Western Europe. The modern nation of France derives its name from the Franks.

79: **well-stoked:** referring to a fireplace containing a well-built fire

80 **dispelleth:** dispels, or scatters, gets rid of

81 **Morpheus:** Ancient Greek god of dreams, here described as a slow river that flows into the sleeper's mind.

82 **nightfold:** literally, a fenced area where a flock of sheep are kept safe at night; figuratively, the sense of safety and comfort one feels when tucked into bed at night.

[*BOTH sing.*]
> A light we espy…

[*CHOIR sings, from without.*]
> From the Frankish castle beam'd forth

BOTH
> A light we espy…

CHOIR
> From its well-stoked flaming hearth.

BOTH
> A light we espy, a light,
> That dispelleth the dark in every life.

RIFF-RAFF [*Sings, from without.*]
> Down from the river darkness passage streams,
> flow Morpheus, slow, that carries nightfold's dreams.
> Let gloom give way to Sun and glowing light
> and may my life, O my life, shine as bright.

BOTH
> A light we espy…

CHOIR
> From the Frankish castle beam'd forth

BOTH
> A light we espy…

CHOIR
> From its well-stoked flaming hearth.

83 **pithy:** concise and direct

84 **mine:** my

85 **cotter-pins:** pegs or folded pins, much like bobby-pins in shape, used to secure wheels in place on an axle

BOTH
> *A light we espy, a light,*
> *that dispelleth the dark in every life.*

BRAD
Now our song it is ended.

GROUNDLING
Good!

BRAD
Once more kick I this wheel
for it did fail us in our hour of need.
And, leaving it, as it did leave our carriage,
we shall take ourselves to yon castle near.

JANET
But what of the sign's pithy warning?

GROUNDLING
Huh. She said "pithy"!

GENTLEWOMAN
I do "pithy" you, sirrah, as it seems
you want of schooling.

GROUNDLING
Whuh?

BRAD
Ne'er was I one to take heed of such things.
For example, mine lowly manservant
did advise me to replace the cotter-pins
on my carriage, though they were but little worn.

86 **impertinence:** presumptuousness. The servant was not
actually impertinent. Brad here displays a tendency to blame and
punish those who try to help him by pointing out small problems
before they become big ones.

87 **fourpence:** four measly cents. Run, Janet, run. Brad's not only
abusive, but a cheap bastard, and short-sighted to boot.

88 **Dame Fortuna:** the personification of Fortune, or luck, both
good and bad

89 **plight:** bad situation

90 **knavish:** mischievous

91 **attend:** Pay attention to

I beat him soundly for his impertinence, and, so doing,
saved myself fourpence on new pins
by not buying them.

JANET
And what cost you the carriage and the wheel?

BRAD
Hush, Janet. This muddy road is not the place
to speak on't. Let us to the castle haste.

Enter THE BARD.

THE BARD
And so it was Dame Fortuna smil'd
'pon Sir Brad and Janet, soft and mild.
Assistance in their evening's plight she granted
upon them: a door, a roof, a fire, a bed.
Yet this is not the happy end you think,
for Fortune she doth cast a knavish wink.
Dear friends, Fortune's fools they yet may be.
Attend what follows, and you soon shall see.

Exeunt.

92 **Beelzebub:** the high god Ba'al Zebul of the Philistines of the ancient city of Ekron, in the land of Canaan. Beelzebub appears to be a Hebrew derogatory corruption of this name, heavy with sarcasm and implying that Beelzebub is not a god but a demon, closely associated with Satan.

93 **singular:** curious, strange

Riff-Raff.

SCENE 3. – Frank N. Furter's Castle.

Foyer, seen inside and out.

BRAD and JANET arrive at castle door.

JANET
O fearsome walls! I tremble at their sight.
Let us away and elsewhere sleep this night.

BRAD
I'll not tarry longer in this damp gale. [*Knocks.*]

Enter Riff-Raff, opposing.

RIFF-RAFF
Here's a knocking, indeed! [*Knocking without.*]
Knock, knock, knock!
Who's there, I' the name of Beelzebub?

BRAD
Lord Brad and Lady Janet. Prithee, sirrah, open!

RIFF-RAFF
Brad and Janet? Singular names, aye.

BRAD
Hurry! We are soaking wet!

RIFF-RAFF
Now you be Soak and Whit? Also singular names!
What 'ave ye done wi' Brad and Janet?

94 **naught:** nothing

95 **ope:** Open

96 **breach:** opening or weak spot

BRAD
We have done naught with Brad and Janet!
We *are* Brad and Janet! [*Knocks.*]
Come, for we are drenched through and through!

JANET
O fool! We are but lost travelers, caught by storm.
Ope this door at once!

RIFF-RAFF
I hear a woman's tones! Pray, be you Soak or Whit?

JANET
Neither; I am Janet.

RIFF-RAFF
Tonight, the castle doth do the ladies honor.
First glass is on the house.

BRAD
Ope this door, or, by God, I'll break it down!
[*Heaves against door.*]

                                        GENTLEMAN
                            Once more unto the breach!

RIFF-RAFF opens the door. BRAD enters all a-tumble.
JANET enters in a manner usual.

RIFF-RAFF
Come, come! Tarry not i' the door-way –
'Tis foul without.

97 **borne:** carried or conveyed

98 **raiment ... damp sheep:** Brad's clothes smell pretty bad due to the rain. His kilt must be made of wool, which, until the practice of treating it with petroleum distillates was developed in the late 19th Century, retained traces of natural oils which gave off a rank odor when wet.

99 **shew:** show, spoken as a rustic

BRAD
Know you, sirrah, that I am Brad,
of the House of Majors, of Denton;
a gentleman born.

RIFF-RAFF
Perhaps a gentleman born, but not a gentleman borne.
It seems you have muddied your boots with walking,
and your raiment doth reek of damp sheep.

JANET
Our carriage did a wheel lose in the wood,
good sir. We wish only a fire, a dry bed,
and safe passage upon the morn.

RIFF-RAFF
You're soaking wet.

JANET
Aye.

GROUNDLING
Why?

JANET
'Tis raining.

GROUNDLING
Good reason. Can't be because of Brad.

Lightning from without,
illuminating Carriages.

RIFF-RAFF
Come hither. Dry quarters will I shew you.

100 **the lord doth keep his revels:** He's throwing a party

101 **blest:** blessed

JANET
O Brad, what manner of place be this?
Thy father's own mansion doth not
so formidable look, nor chill the bone so.

BRAD
Perhaps 'tis a hunting-lodge for the lord
and his chosen guests, built to please his tastes
for the season, with no thought given
to inhabitation for the full of the year.

GENTLEMAN
Methinks his lordship's tastes do run
through channels most rich and strange.

RIFF-RAFF
Hither. Guests, you have arrived on a night
most auspicious, for the lord doth keep his revels here,
and two more will all the merrier his table make.

JANET
Good grace to your lord, then, so by Fortune blest!

Enter MAGENTA.

MAGENTA
So, too, are you by Fortune blest!
You're blest, he's blest, I'm blest,
we all of us are blest! [*Laughs.*]

Enter TRANSYLVANIANS, THE BARD and COLUMBIA.
Enter Musicians, opposed and playing "Time's Warp and Weft".

102 **Phaeton's charge:** Phaeton's wild ride. In Greek mythology, a son of Apollo. He borrowed his father's chariot of the Sun but couldn't control it and nearly set the word ablaze.

Phaëton, driving in the manner of a Jackass.

103 **trip the shore:** step upon the surface of, as though arriving as a shore after a sea voyage

104 **humors:** more ancient Greek influence! Hippocrates (ca. 460-370 BCE) is credited with developing the idea of four bodily humors, or fluids, an imbalance of which could cause emotional upset. They were: blood, yellow bile, black bile, and phlegm. Since hormones weren't discovered until 1902 (English physician E.H. Starling and physiologist W.M. Bayliss), and neuroreceptors even later, the four humors idea persisted through, and well beyond, Shakespeare's time.

105 **Time's Warp and Weft:** Warp and weft are the horizontal and vertical threads of woven cloth. This song concerns the fabric of Time.

106 **steps and measure:** dance steps, and how the music goes. In music, a "measure" is a set duration of beats, used to break the music into manageable chunks for learning and to make clear the rhythmic pattern.

107 **tip:** touch the tops of

RIFF-RAFF [*Sings.*]
> *Since last I saw home, these many years,*
> *madness hath, like Phaeton's charge,*
> *come near to scorching the hills and vales*
> *of my brain.*

MAGENTA [*Sings.*]
> *Our suff'ring soon shall end,*
> *when we once more*
> *do trip the shore*
> *of home, all ills will mend.*

RIFF-RAFF
> *Mine humors must I restrain.*
> *I recall how we danced 'pon purple sands,*
> *'neath pale moons and familiar stars,*
> *yea, the old dance, of Time's Warp and Weft!*
> *Well knew we the steps and measure,*
> *and until dawn's green light did tip the trees*
> *would savor the sweet deeps of darkness*

BOTH
> *And surrender to the calling void...*

ALL TRANSYLVANIANS, RIFF-RAFF and MAGENTA
> *Prithee the frolic begin!*
> *Time's Warp and Weft weave again!*

GENTLEMAN
Instruct us in this dance, O Bard!

108 **a sprightly leftward leap:** Oh, come on! Even the groundlings know this one.

109 ***Et trois Côté droit!:*** ...And three balletic steps to the right, *s'il vous plais.*

110 **taut:** tight

111 **in attitude rude:** in a sexually suggestive manner

112 **ken:** scrutiny or understanding

113 **cowslip's ear:** the flower of a cowslip

A Cowslip.

THE BARD
Commence Time's Warp and Weft
With but a sprightly leftward leap.
                    Music stops.

                                        GROUNDLING
                    You mean, it's just a jump to the left?

THE BARD
Grant this Groundling free admission!
'Tis but a jump to the left!

        Music resumes. ALL dance, save BRAD and JANET,
                who comprehendeth not.

ALL
        Et trois Côté droit!

THE BARD
        On thy hips plant thy hands!

ALL
        And draw thy knees in taut!
        Thy pelvis move in attitude rude
        that seize the brain besides the heart!
        Prithee the frolic begin!
        Time's Warp and Weft weave again!

MAGENTA
        On the light fantastic toe
        afloat on moonlight beams I go
        to world beyond the one you know,
        beyond the ken of mortal men.
        In a cowslip's ear I lie,
        hidden well from mortal eye,

114 **firmament celestial:** celestial firmament, or the night sky

115 **transcendental:** going beyond everyday matters or concerns

116 **a-Maying:** enjoying the fine May weather

117 **Laird:** a Scottish lord

118 **gay:** <sigh> Again, not what you think. Cheerful and brightly-colored

119 **culled:** cut and gathered

Columbia.

> *secluded thus, from there I spy;*
> *they see not me, yet I see all.*

RIFF-RAFF
> *It takes but a turn of the mind...*

MAGENTA
> *To leave this planet behind...*

RIFF-RAFF
> *We have had years to master this art.*

MAGENTA
> *Through the firmament celestial*

RIFF-RAFF
> *In trance transcendental!*

ALL
> *Prithee the frolic begin!*
> *Time's Warp and Weft weave again!*

COLUMBIA [*To the tune of "Early One Morning"*]
> *As I went out a-Maying, one bright and dewy morning,*
> *the Laird of this Castle he did overtake my mare.*
> *Black the steed that he did ride, black the gems that were*
> *his eyes.*
> *He stared and winked, I trembled so, and Time did flee, and*
> *grief, and woe.*
> *Gay is the garland, fresh are the roses*
> *I've culled from the garden to bind around his crown.*

ALL
> *Prithee the frolic begin!*
> *Time's Warp and Weft weave again!*

THE BARD
'Tis but a jump to the left!

ALL
    Et trois Côté droit!

THE BARD
    On thy hips plant thy hands!

ALL
    And draw thy knees in taut!
    Thy pelvis move in attitude rude
    that seize the brain besides the heart!
    Prithee the frolic begin!
    Time's Warp and Weft weave again!

        COLUMBIA dances a merry Jig.

ALL
    Prithee the frolic begin!
    Time's Warp and Weft weave again!

THE BARD
    'Tis but a jump to the left!

ALL
    Et trois Côté droit!

THE BARD
    On thy hips plant thy hands!

ALL
    And draw thy knees in taut!

120 **Huzzah!:** Hooray!

121 **galliard:** a lively dance in ¾ time, popular during the Renaissance

122 **turn a merry courant:** dance awhile; cut a rug

123 **gimlets:** daggers

Thy pelvis move in attitude rude
that seize the brain besides the heart!
Prithee the frolic begin!
Time's Warp and Weft weave again!
Huzzah!

> *ALL the Dancers collapse on the flags,*
> *quite spent.*

JANET
Brad, stand not amazed! Speak, man!

BRAD
I know not the steps of this new dance.
But play me a galliard, that I may turn
a merry courant with my lady.

> *ALL the Dancers slowly rise,*
> *staring gimlets at BRAD and JANET.*

GENTLEMAN
Let us all remain standing, to honor
His Majesty, the Queen!

> *Enter DOCTOR FRANK N. FURTER, clothed as a woman*
> *of the loosest morals.*

GROUNDLING
That strumpet's a man!

GENTLEMAN
You, sirrah, are as devoid of sense as…

GROUNDLING
Look, see? – She's a man!

124 **T'would be a scandal:** Yep, in Shakespeare's day, women weren't allowed to perform on stage. That's right. Juliet was played by a dude, bro.

125 **lechery:** in this case, shame at the sight

126 **fast:** tight

127 **revel:** party

128 **Whither away?:** Where to?

129 **brakes:** bushes; forested parts

GENTLEMAN
Well, did you expect otherwise?
T'would be a scandal for a woman to take the stage.

GENTLEWOMAN
My nursemaid always was wont to say,
"Life upon the wicked stage ain't nothing for a girl."

JANET
O monstrous! I must hide mine eyes for very lechery.
The very sight of this man doth my humors
put all out of order.

BRAD
'Zounds, Janet, to thine own self hold fast.
'Tis merely a revel. Methinks
the liquor did flow perhaps too freely.
T'will do no damage here that the Sun,
upon the morn, will not make repair'd.

JANET
Brad, nay! We must fly – I wish it so!

BRAD
Whither away? We know not these wild brakes.

JANET
Ask the porter; mayhap he would know
of other lodgings we may take.

BRAD
This bacchanal hath taken on the form
of a rite. Soft, Janet; we must not interfere.

JANET
This be no church; no holy mass wilt thou disrupt,

130 **bacchanal:** a particularly wild revel, with strong drink. In this case, a play on words, since Bacchus was the Roman god of wine and also of theater. The Bacchantes, or devotees of his temple, carried out mystical rituals with Masonic secrecy. (Doesn't sound like a wild party to me, but that's the paradox of it all.)

131 **mark their garments:** Notice how they're dressed.

132 **doth run much counter to:** is different from

133 **Hark!:** Listen!

no God displease, if you but whisper in
the porter's ear.

BRAD
They may be of lands foreign to us.
Mark their garments; the cut of their cloths
doth run much counter to our own.
No, we cannot guess as to their ways.
But – Hark! The musicians strike up again.
Methinks I know the paces of this dance.

JANET
O mockery! Fie upon you! Fie!
Cold and wet, I stand here still,
and would I fain be feather-dry!
My teeth do clack, my bones are chill,
my fever'd brow portends of ill,
and greatly all afear'd am I.

BRAD
I'm here. Be not afear'd!

FRANK [*Sings.*]
>   *I bid thee welcome, soggy ones,*
>   *to my castle, dry as bones.*
>   *My aide-de-camp you've met, I ween.*
>   *Do you pardon his flippant tongue,*
>   *his jibes and fleers when bell you rung –*
>   *The sweetmeat man whom children sung*
>   *he'd been expecting of the e'en.*
>
>   *Art thou by my look out-strung?*
>   *Judge a book's text, not what's sung*
>   *writ upon its cover alone.*
>   *Daylight does not my form flatter,*
>   *perhaps, but such things do not matter*

134 *aide-de-camp*: right-hand man. Literally, a knight's squire, or assistant in battle

135 **flippant:** disrespectful

136 **sweetmeat:** candy (although usually consisting of fruit and nuts, so we'd think of it as health food or trail mix)

137 **galliards and voltes of sprightly mien:** dances of the lively sort

138 **theatrics in Hercules' vein:** feats of strength. This may be a reference to the pagan rite known as Festivus (for the rest of us), indicating that Doctor Faustus Frank N. Furter is perhaps a heretic, marking him as a villainous figure in the theatre of Shakespeare's time.

when night doth fall and Moon grow fatter...
I am a lover, of great renown!

Resplendent I am, in women's garb!
From my shoulders' beam hang silken scarve.
Skirts billow o'er my hips and bum.
From Transsexual, Transylvania I come.
[*Dances.*]

GENTLEWOMAN
This young fellow is the least
convincing woman I hath ever seen.

GENTLEMAN
That is the intent, for he portrays
a man who dresseth as a woman.

GROUNDLING
That's what I meant! ...I think.

FRANK
My castle holds delights in plenty;
we lack for naught in entertainment. We
have musicians to tickle thine ears
with galliards and voltes of sprightly mien.
Or we can please you in Hercules' vein

GENTLEMAN
Or artery!

FRANK
With theatrics to tear a cat in twain.
Whatever you will, we'll do, my dears!

Doctor Faustus
Frank N. Furter.

BRAD
We need a swift rider –
or runner provided –
to dispatch a brief note to our master.

JANET
'Tis true.

BRAD
You need not make fuss
to entertain us.
Our carriage in woods pitched a caster.

FRANK
> *On forest path thy carriage lies;*
> *hardly cause for much surprise.*
> *Accidents here are commonality.*
> *You needn't act so puritanical;*
> *I'll furnish you with rude mechanical*
> *whose skills might seem to some Satanical,*
> *whilst you enjoy my hospitality.*
>
> *Resplendent I am, in women's garb!*
> *From my shoulders' beam hang silken scarve.*
> *Skirts billow o'er my hips and bum.*
> *From Transsexual, Transylvania I come.*
>
> *I must insist you stay the night.*

RIFF-RAFF
Night.

139 **victuals:** food

140 **repair:** retreat; take a look at

FRANK
> *I've victuals to tempt your appetite.*

COLUMBIA
Appetite.

FRANK
> *I set forth a bounteous table.*
> *But first we shall to my cell repair,*
> *where a man, full-formed and fair of hair,*
> *with cheek of tan and feet all bare,*
> *I've made, and will with life enable!*
>
> *Resplendent I am, in women's garb!*
> *From my shoulders' beam hang silken scarve.*
> *Skirts billow o'er my hips and bum.*

ALL
Hips and bum...

FRANK
> *From Transsexual...*

COLUMBIA, RIFF-RAFF and MAGENTA
Transylvania!

GROUNDLING
Tell us what you do when you see a fair man, Frank!

FRANK
> *... I come.*
>
> *I bid thee join me in my cell*
> *and there behold what there do dwell*

141 **a slab of marble hewn:** a slab carved from marble

142 **ablate causation:** lessen or remove the cause

143 *Exeunt omnes*: They all leave

upon a slab of marble hewn.
You shiver from antici...

GENTLEMAN
Speak, man! ... If man thou be.

FRANK
 ...pation?

BRAD and JANET
No, Milord; in faith, we're soaking wet!

FRANK
My servants will for thee some dry clothes get. [*Claps hands.*]

 Exeunt RIFF-RAFF and MAGENTA.

FRANK
Where was I?
 Ah! You shake from precipitation.
 Dry clothing will ablate causation;
 still you'll quake to think what you'll be shewn!

JANET
We accept your gracious offer, Milord.

BRAD
Our thanks it is beyond measure.

 Exeunt omnes.

144 **I am unaccustomed ... myself:** Upper-class people of the time kept servants who sometimes assisted their masters and mistresses in the complicated tasks of dressing and undressing.

145 **stays:** devices, usually ribbons, used to hold articles of clothing shut together

146 **codpiece:** a leather pouch fitted at the crotch of a man's trousers, hose or breeches. Yep, a "nut hut". In some places and times, these might get rather big and elaborate.

A Codpiece.

ACT II.

SCENE 1. – *A Room in Dr. Frank N. Furter's Castle. Enter BRAD and JANET.*

JANET
I am unaccustomed to dressing myself.
I shall require thy assistance, Brad,
in unfastening my stays.

BRAD
A task I will happily undertake,
if thou but assist in the removal of my codpiece.

> GENTLEMAN
> Methinks they both want of practice!

JANET
Although I am grateful for the use
of their fire, I am yet troubled.
Have you given thought to leaving yet?

BRAD
Faith, stay here this night; they will
surely do us no harm.

JANET
I will not stay to-night for all the town.
Darkness and the gloomy shade of death
environ this place.

147 **for the nonce:** for the time being; at this time

148 **meet:** appropriate

149 **fetch thee anon:** bring you soon

150 **cell:** The word "laboratory" does not appear in the literature of the time. Alchemists (early chemists) worked in cells, or private rooms.

151 **crucibles and alembics:** laboratory equipment, still used today by chemists.

Crucible & Alembic.

152 **deem:** consider

153 **Titus Andronicus:** A Roman general and subject of another play by Shakespeare, considered his most bloody and violent. At one point, Titus' sons are wrongly imprisoned and sentenced to die, and he is forced to ransom them by cutting off his own right hand.
Titus Andronicus is usually not covered, or even mentioned, in high school Literature classes. Evelyn Nesbitt even declined to give it a place in her book *Beautiful Stories from Shakespeare for Children* (1907).

BRAD
Well enough, milady.
We shall bide our time for the nonce,
then make good our escape in
the fullness of time.
When playing at cards, 'tis not meet
to show one's hand premature.

Enter COLUMBIA, MAGENTA and RIFF-RAFF.

COLUMBIA
If thou bidest thy time, good sir,
then do so when unfastening the lady's stays.
'Tis too fine a job to warrant haste.

BRAD
I am Brad Majors, a gentleman of Denton town.
This damsel is Janet Weiss, my betrothed.
Hast come to attend to our chamber?

COLUMBIA
Nay; we are come to fetch thee anon.
Our lord bids thee attend to his labors
in his cell.
And there, upon a slab of marble made,
will you see that which hath emerged
from his busy crucibles and alembics.
This invitation is extended to few indeed;
you may deem yourselves fortunate.
Many would give, like Titus Andronicus of old,
their right arm, and ten times as willingly,
for the privilege.

154 **dalliance:** in this case, dilly-dallying; wasting precious time

155 **Avaunt!:** Let's go! Ain't got all night.

Magenta.

BRAD
I must decline the offer, as we have business
elsewhere, and needed only to dry our clothes
and await the daylight.

COLUMBIA
I have with mine own eyes seen this magic,
these wonders alchemical. Had you an inkling
of what awaits, you would hasten with such speed
as to place yourself ahead of me, like an eager dog
who leads his master, tail awag, tongue apant,
though he knows not whither his master would go.

MAGENTA
Enough! Our master has little patience
for dalliance. Dry clothes await you
in his chambers. Avaunt!

JANET [*to MAGENTA*]
Is the lord of this castle your husband?

RIFF-RAFF
The master has not yet taken a wife, nor do I expect
he ever will. We are his humble servants, and nothing more.

Exeunt omnes.

GROUNDLING
Damn, I was hoping he'd undo those stays.

GENTLEWOMAN
Likewise, in the matter of that codpiece.

156 **cauldron:** cooking-pot

157 **flagon of ale:** brewski. A flagon is a large drinking vessel, roughly 1.1 L in volume. Ale is a beer with a bitter flavor and higher alcoholic content than other beers.

158 **chemises:** undergarments of inexpensive, plain fabric, resembling nightshirts

SCENE 2. – *DR. FRANK N. FURTER'S Cell.*
A large Cauldron is placed central.

Enter BRAD and JANET, now in their undergarments,
with RIFF-RAFF, COLUMBIA and MAGENTA,
and DR. FRANK N. FURTER, opposed.
RIFF-RAFF gives DR. FRANK N. FURTER a Flagon of Ale.
MAGENTA gives DR. FRANK N. FURTER two Chemises.

> GENTLEMAN
> To your health, master – I hope you choke!

FRANK
Mistress Magenta, Columbia – go, and assist Riff-Raff
in his ministrations. It will be my pleasure
to entertain our unexpected guests myself.
I beg pardon; your names escape me.

Exeunt RIFF-RAFF, COLUMBIA and MAGENTA.

BRAD
I am Brad Majors, a gentleman of Denton town.
This damsel is Janet Vice, my betrothèd.
That is, Weiss.

JANET
'Tis Weiss.

BRAD
Aye, 'tis Weiss.

> GENTLEWOMAN
> What a fool this Brad be!

159 **clime:** climate

160 **proffer:** offer

161 **sixpence:** six cents. Adjusting for inflation, probably over $75 in today's lousy economy.

162 **niggardly:** I know, I know – it sounds racist. It isn't. It means "stingy" and is from Old English *hneaw*, meaning "stingy". Brad would seriously treat Janet to a Motel 6 and try to tell her it was the Hilton.

163 **I am pleased...:** I would prefer...

GENTLEMAN
Neither wise nor Weiss.

FRANK
In the manner of the Frenchmen,
Enchanté. I am well pleased
to make your acquaintance.
Your undergarments are most charming,
but unsuited to this chilly clime. Here,
put these on, that you may feel less vulnerable.
Forgive my manners; visitors to this castle
are infrequent, and unaccustomed are we,
as consequence, to proffer hospitality.
[*He gives them the Chemises.*]

JANET dons her Chemise.
BRAD casts his to the Floor.

BRAD
That which you call hospitality
I call most doubtful, sir.
We did but ask little –
a fire, a bed for the night –
no more nor less than one could
expect at an inn for sixpence.

GENTLEWOMAN
Sixpence? How niggardly
this Brad be as well!

BRAD
Yet you do wrong us
by ignoring our request most reasonable.
If that be hospitality, sir,
I am pleased not to recognize it.

164 **paragon:** the best

165 **marks ... made by mortal hands:** birthmarks or tattoos

A Mark made by mortal Hand.

JANET
Brad, be not ungrateful.

BRAD
Ungrateful! Methinks the lowest servant
worthy of more courtesy than we've been shewn.
We, who are your guests, and lost travelers beside.

FRANK
I stand amazèd at thy virility,
O Brad.

GENTLEMAN
Methinks Frank's virility does stand, as well!

FRANK
What a piece of work is this man.
How dominant in nature.
In form and moving, how express and admirable!
The paragon of animals!
Proud of him might you well be, Lady Janet.

JANET
Indeed, I am.

FRANK
Brad, have you any blemishes?
Any marks of birth, or made by mortal hand?

BRAD
Marry, I do not!

BRAD dons his Chemise.

GROUNDLING
Show him the one with the dancing bear, Brad!

166 **ere:** before

167 **Helios will ascend:** The Sun will rise. In Greek mythology, Helios was the Sun. In some myths, he was equated with Apollo; in others, Apollo was his chauffeur.

168 **effulgent:** gaudy; showy

169 **Hyperion:** a Titan, father of Helios

170 **sausage:** A reference to the proverb, "If one enjoys sausage, one should not ask how it was made." There is, of course, a sexual double entendre here.

171 **by dint of:** by means of

FRANK
Verily so. Do you, Lady Janet?

JANET
Forsooth!

Enter RIFF-RAFF, followed by COLUMBIA,
MAGENTA and TRANSYLVANIANS..

RIFF-RAFF
All is in readiness, master.
Now we await only your word.

FRANK
Very well. Friends, Transylvanians, countrymen –
lend me your ears.
This night shall see a miracle rare,
a dream made palpable, to ope the gates
of Paradise itself ere dawn arrives!
Helios will ascend, only to bow
before my creation, effulgent in splendor.
My labors' fruit shall the very Sun outshone,
and make of me a newly-crown'd Hyperion!
And yet, it humbles me to think on't.
How came this thing to pass?

                              GENTLEMAN
                    Now Frank will tell us how
                        the sausage was made.

FRANK
T'was not by dint of design,
laid out in perfect wholeness
like an architect's plans, no equation
resolv'd on paper ere it was made flesh.
My brains I racked for many a tiresome year
to no avail. Then, by pure chance,

172 **beggar'd:** poor

173 **Jovian bolt:** lightning, as used by Jupiter, or Jove, chief of the Roman gods

Jove, with a Bolt.

174 **arcane:** secret; mysterious

175 **homunculus:** a living man, usually small, created from inanimate matter by a sorcerer

176 **a nascence momentous ... woke:** a birth as important as that of Adam, the first man, when he awoke in the Garden of Eden where he was created. (Judeo-Christian mythology, also well-known to Shakespeare's audience)

177 **censers:** incense-burners

178 **Greasy Joan:** a surprisingly well-remembered name from Shakespeare's comedy *Love's Labours Lost*, although she's not a character. She is mentioned in a song about winter, sung at a party at the end of the play. Keeling the pot (stirring a cauldron of hot soup) is what she does best.

the pattern emerged, simple even in
its very intricacies. O beggar'd fool I was,
not to have seen it! By one small accident,
I laid bare the discovery that hath philosophers eluded
since time past telling. An accident!
And thus discovered I the missing element,
the Jovian bolt, the heavenly fire
that is the breath of life.
Aye, that mystery, that arcane knowledge
is mine, and mine alone. That secret
to life itself.

GENTLEWOMAN
'Tis more than I wished to know.

FRANK
See now, good friends,
and Fortune praise, for you shall soon bear witness
to the birth of my homunculus,
my beautiful creature.
Aye, a nascence momentous
as that of Adam when upon Eden's loam he woke.
Such a new dawn shall you see break forth.
In my deep-vaulted cell the charm I'll prepare.
Riff-Raff, do the censers set alight.
Magenta, upon my shoulders my cloak of magic place.
Columbia, attend the cauldron.
Greasy Joan, come hither! [*Claps hands.*]

GENTLEMAN
Greasy Joan! Greasy Joan!

Enter GREASY JOAN.

179 **My part ... discharged.:** My work here is done.

180 **allay:** put away

Greasy Joan doth keel the Pot.

> GENTLEWOMAN
> 'Tis Greasy Joan herself!
> I knew not she were in this play.

FRANK
Greasy Joan, do keel the pot.

> *GREASY JOAN doth keel the Pot.*

GREASY JOAN
My part I have discharged.

> *Exit GREASY JOAN.*

> GENTLEMAN
> Well keeled, Greasy Joan! Well keeled!

> GENTLEWOMAN
> Well keeled! Oh, Greasy Joan
> doth excel in ev'ry play she's in.

JANET
O Brad, much afeared am I!

BRAD
Allay thy fear, for I am here.

> GENTLEMAN
> Brad speaks bold words;
> but I hope he hath brought
> a change of undergarment!

COLUMBIA
Master, the essence hath congealed!

181 **drab:** a plug-ugly woman

A Drab.

FRANK
Eye of lizard, wing of bat,
tongue of newt, this and that!

COLUMBIA
Master, a skeleton hath formed!

GROUNDLING
He's got a boner already?
Guy wastes no time!

FRANK
Finger cut from a birth-strangled babe
ditch-delivered by a drab!

COLUMBIA
Master, he reaches forth with hands of flesh!
Nails tip his fingers. Eyes roll in his head,
and teeth and tongue do fill his mouth.

FRANK
Need he more fingers cut from birth-strangled babe?

COLUMBIA
Nay; he be complete.

FRANK
Nine more have I, cut fresh of yesternight.
Upon the morrow they will begin to stink.

COLUMBIA
Very well, then. One more.

182 **I've spake the rune:** I've spoken the charm

183 **what-not:** I'll give you one guess.

184 **loins:** ...And there's your answer.

185 **Sword of Damocles:** In Greek mythology, Damocles was an admirer of Dionysius II, tyrant king of Syracuse (4th Century BCE – "tyrant" in this case simply means he was not in the line of succession to the throne and took over by other means, such as a military coup. He may have been a good king.). Anyway, Damocles felt that Dionysius enjoyed a cushy life of endless comfort. So Dionysius let Damocles be king for a day. While Damocles enjoyed a lavish party, he looked up and saw a heavy sword hanging by a thread over his head. Dionysius explained that it is the sword of responsibility that hangs over the head of every king. One bad decision, and the thread may break.

The Sword of Damocles.

186 **Sisters Three:** the Three Fates in Greek mythology, who cut the threads representing everyone's lives. A bit of a mixed metaphor, I know. Bear with me. 'Tis but a play.

FRANK
By tempest blast,
the spell is cast.
By Sun and Moon,
I've spake the rune.
Come out, come out, come out the pot.
Columbia, conceal thou his what-not.

> *ROCKY emerges naked from the Cauldron.*
> *COLUMBIA drapes his loins.*

GENTLEMAN
Though 'tis midnight, the bawdy hand of
Frank's dial is now upon the prick of noon.

FRANK
O Rocky! A most high miracle!

ROCKY
I am born.
[*Sings.*]
> *The Sword of Damocles, it hangeth above my head,*
> *and now I have a sense of inescapable dread.*
> *Though I yet wake*
> *my soul is well-deep with ache.*
> *The fear I take*
> *Is the Sisters Three, cutting thread on a counter.*

ALL
> *Allay, allay, allay thy fear.*
> *No crime hast thou committed here.*

GENTLEMAN
Only a crime against theater!

187 **wrack:** to shake; to throttle

ROCKY

A dream I had of like to wrack me in my bed.

ALL

Allay, allay, allay thy fear.
No crime hast thou committed here.

ROCKY

Whither up? Whither down?
One is like to th' other.
Richly cloth'd, from foot to crown,
yet I sense I needn't bother.

GENTLEWOMAN
True; with clothes thou needn't bother!

ALL

Fa-la-la-la
Allay, allay, allay thy fear.
No crime hast thou committed here.

ROCKY

Derry-down, derry-down...

ALL

Fa-la-la-la
Allay, allay, allay thy fear.
No crime hast thou committed here.

ROCKY

Derry-down, derry-down...

ALL

Fa-la-la-la
Allay, allay, allay thy fear.
No crime hast thou committed here.

188 **rings:** runs arounds in circles

ROCKY
> *Derry-down, derry-down*
> *E'en now I have a sense of looming dread,*

ALL
> *Allay, allay, allay thy fear.*
> *No crime hast thou committed here.*

ROCKY
> *For the Sword of Damocles hangs above my head.*

ALL
> *Allay, allay, allay thy fear.*
> *No crime hast thou committed here.*

ROCKY
> *Although I am begun to wake*
> *my soul is nigh well-deep with ache,*
> *and I fear the Sisters Three may cut the thread.*

FRANK
O Rocky!

> *FRANK pursues ROCKY, who rings the Cell*
> *in terror. Singing continues.*

ALL
> *Fa-la-la-la*
> *Allay, allay, allay thy fear.*
> *No crime hast thou committed here.*

ROCKY
> *Derry-down, derry-down...*

ALL

> *Fa-la-la-la*
> *Allay, allay, allay thy fear.*
> *No crime hast thou committed here.*

ROCKY

Derry-down, derry-down...

ALL

> *Fa-la-la-la*
> *Allay, allay, allay thy fear.*
> *No crime hast thou committed here.*

ROCKY

> *Derry-down, derry-down...*

ALL

> *Fa-la-la-la*
> *Allay, allay, allay thy fear.*
> *No crime hast thou committed here.*

ROCKY

> *Derry-down, derry-down...*

ALL

> *Fa-la-la-la*
> *Allay, allay, allay thy fear.*
> *No crime hast thou committed here.*
> *Fa-la-la-la-la!*

> *FRANK seizes ROCKY. Song ends.*

FRANK

Rocky, forsooth! You flee from one
who means you no harm.

GROUNDLING
But it might hurt for a while!

FRANK
If I pursue thee, it is from admiration.
Your behavior on your first day
is most unseemly.

ROCKY
I weep, I know not why.

FRANK
Be yet of good cheer. Thy beauty
is exceptional. I forgive thee.

ROCKY
I laugh, I know not why.

FRANK
O Success! Thy name is Rocky.

RIFF-RAFF
A credit to your genius this homunculus be, Master.

FRANK
Yes.

MAGENTA
A triumph of your will.

FRANK
Yes.

COLUMBIA
Methinks he be adequate.

189 **atom:** In Shakespeare's day, the concept of an atom was still in keeping with that of the Greek philosopher Democritus (400 BCE), who posited that all matter was composed of indestructible and irreducible units. The idea of elements being composed of single materials and therefore the same atoms came along with the chemist John Dalton in 1803.

190 **zephyr:** a gentle breeze

191 **Hercules and the Nemean Lion:** Hercules, or Herakles in Greek, is, of course, the mythical strong-man. The Nemean Lion was a beast that he slew bare-handed.

192 **Atlas:** a Titan, giant from Greek mythology, who was condemned to hold the sky upon his shoulders. He once tricked Hercules into relieving him of his burden; but Hercules tricked him into taking it back.

193 **starveling of but seven soft stone:** a weakling weighing 98 pounds (441 N, or 45 Kg). A "stone", therefore, was a unit of weight equal to 14 pounds.

FRANK
But adequate? [*FRANK strikes COLUMBIA.*]
Merely adequate?
Surely can'st speak higher praise than that!
Doubtless our guests marvel at the wonder
unveil'd here this night. Pray, Brad and Janet,
speak! What humors stir within your breast
upon beholding Rocky?

JANET
Forgive me; 'tis not my intent
to disparage thy Lordship's work.
But I find men o'er-wrought with muscles,
well-marbled though they be, and like unto a cake of beef,
not to my liking.

FRANK
I created him not... for you!
Every atom of his being is of my choosing,
to suit my appetites. I prefer
a man with pillar-like strength,
whose sinews ripple as he moves.
Yes, ripple like a brook stirred by a zephyr,
yet possess the savage might of a tempest!
Hercules and the Nemean lion, all in one.
Hercules, who did once take 'pon the hills of his shoulders
the dome of the heavens from Atlas himself.
Aye, Atlas. And the titan did grudgingly approve
the hero's strength and shrewdness.
Musicians, attend.
[*Sings.*]
>   *A starveling of but seven soft stone*
>   *will taste of sand upon which he is thrown.*
>   *And hence he must, with weak-formed chin outthrust,*
>   *by lifting he doth make his form robust.*

194 **glister:** glisten

195 **the Hebrew God ... seven days:** a further reference to the story of Adam, who was created from clay on the sixth of the seven days it took God to make the world.

196 **Dynamic tension:** while wrestling is famously included in his comedy *As You Like It*, and the hammer-throw and bar-bell were both staples of physical exercise in Shakespeare's time as they are now, Frank here lets slip a clue as to his extraterrestrial provenance. Dynamic Tension would not reach our globe until the 20th Century, when Charles Atlas established his exercise program. It consists of a formalized combination of calisthenics and self-resistance, relying on movement. When employed regularly, it works quite well!

197 **anneal:** to make strong

His pores do pucker with liquid fire
as he hoists the iron higher,
and glister his golden torso warm,
the hollows and hills of his sculpted form!
Bath'd in rose-water, like the soft-centered bud of May,
and honey-smooth, he will be a strong man...

ALL

But he will be the wrong man.

FRANK

I will fine meats for him acquire.

GROUNDLING
I bet you will!

FRANK

The hen's raw eggs he'll swallow entire.
Such foundation we'll build upon
to increase his bulk and brawn.
Like the Hebrew God, with lifeless clay,
I'll make of him, in seven days...

ALL

A man, take him for all in all.

FRANK

At mastery of sports he will excel –
wrestling, hammer-throw, the bar-bell.
Dynamic tension will temper the steel
of his vitals, and his humors anneal.
Like the Hebrew God, with lifeless clay,
I'll make of thee, in seven days,
Fa-la-la, fa-la-la, fa-la-lay...
a man, take thee for all in all.

198 **erstwhile:** former

199 **nigh:** near

200 *cap-à-pie*: head-to-foot

201 **severally:** piece-by-piece

202 **the tongs and the bones:** two percussion instruments used in rustic folk music. The bones are still common in Irish and Appalachian folk bands; the tongs are used in Sikh Indian *bhangra* music.

The Tongs and
the Bones.

203 **passing strange:** very strange

204 **ofttimes:** many times

205 **minstrels:** itinerant musicians

206 **crumhorn:** a reed instrument that sounded similar to a saxophone

A Crumhorn.

GENTLEMAN
Music the food of love may be,
But this song hath fed only my appetite.
Columbia, on what shall we dine this e'en?

COLUMBIA
Edward! Young Edward Cutlet!
Our master's erstwhile page-boy. He draws nigh.

Enter EDWARD CUTLET,
clad cap-à-pie in Riding-Apparel,
which he casts off severally.

EDWARD
Musicians! Let us have the tongs and the bones!
And a hey, nonny-nonny –
[*Sings.*]
>Saturday night, O wherefore went away?
>My lady fair in her finest frock did play
>It seemeth not so since summer's day,
>'Twas passing strange, I fancied me God-like.
>Ofttimes we'd ride, my lady and I,
>and listen to the minstrels from the hills on high.
>The crumhorn's sweet notes did Heavenward fly,
>We lay on the heath in dalliance sublime.
>Huzzah! Huzzah! My soul is blest.
>'Tis revels' songs that I love best!
That crumhorn give unto me, quickly!

EDWARD plays the Crumhorn.

208 **porches ... ear:** the porch-like folds of the outer ear, of course

209 **eglantine:** a flower

Eglantine.

210 **lay:** song; ballad

Edward
Cutlet.

EDWARD [*Sings.*]
>   *My lady's sweet perfume did o'erfill*
>   *the caverns of my head, and drive me still*
>   *to greater passions than are meet to tell,*
>   *and she did whisper her troth in porches of mine ear.*
>   *We crown'd our heads with wreaths of eglantine,*
>   *and as the last minstrel his last lay did cry,*
>   *we two sang with him, our arms entwined.*
>   *We lay on the heath in dalliance sublime.*
>   *Huzzah! Huzzah! My soul is blest.*
>   *'Tis revels' songs that I love best!*

FRANK
Once my ear did thrill to the sound of thy sweet voice.
But now to hear you aggrieves me.
This mace shall put a speedy end to thy song.

>   *FRANK pursues EDWARD into an Antechamber.*

EDWARD [*from within*]
Help! Oh, help! Murther!

>   GENTLEMAN
>   Noted thou, how nobody
>   can pronounce "murder"
>   as they are being murdered?

>   GENTLEWOMAN
>   In the terror of the moment,
>   it must be thifficult.

FRANK [*from within*]
Out, vile jelly!

211 **mace:** a short, spiked club

A mace.

212 **murther:** murder. In *Julius Caesar*, Calpurnia awakens from her nightmare crying, "They murther Caesar!", to the confusion of high school kids everywhere.

213 ***Et tu...?:*** Latin for "And you...?" or "You, too...?"

214 **bereft of:** lacking in

215 **mettle:** strength, of body and/or of character

216 **thy head with laurel crown'd:** after the ancient Greek custom of placing a crown of laurel leaves upon a victorious hero's head

A crown of Laurels.

217 **bulwarks:** strong walls, like those protecting a city

EDWARD
Et tu, Faustus?
Then fall poor Edward! I am slain!
[*Dies.*]

FRANK emerges, bloody.

FRANK
One from another deep-vaulted cell.
Magenta, wipe from this mace the stains
of this heavy deed, and call for a light repast.
Let us put it out of thought, for I am grown hungry,
and am of a mind to murder a cutlet.

ROCKY
I know not what to say.

FRANK
O innocent Rocky! Be not forlorn.
A merciful end I gave my onetime page-boy.
Although endowed of certain naïve charm,
young Edward was bereft of brawn.

GENTLEWOMAN
Prithee, Rocky, show us thy fine mettle!

ROCKY poses as for a statue.

FRANK
O Rocky!
> *Thy sinews shaped like Roman marble mound,*
> *thy bosom, hand, thy head with laurel crown'd*
> *doth shake my trem'bling bulwarks to the ground!*

GROUNDLING
Shake those bulwarks!

FRANK
Adam and Atlas, to hold my world in thrall!

ALL
Like the Hebrew God, with lifeless clay,
You'll make of him, in seven days,
a man, take him for all in all.

FRANK
Dynamic tension will temper the steel
of his vitals, and his humors anneal.

JANET
Mere minutes ago, I cared not for brawn.
But now I am pleased to cast eyes upon.

FRANK
Like the Hebrew God, with lifeless clay,
I'll make of thee, in seven days,
Fa-la-la, fa-la-la, fa-la-lay...
I'll make of thee, in seven days,
A man, take thee for all in all.

A Wedding processional.
Exeunt omnes. Enter THE BARD.

THE BARD
Among certain philosophers it is said
that life is illusory –

GROUNDLING
Like your neck!

219 **for all the outrages ... yield no more harm...:** for all the evil things men can do would be as harmless as...

220 **inasmuch as:** as far as

221 **prick:** Not what you think. To "prick" means to stab.

THE BARD
... and that which we call reality,
a mere figment of the imagination.
If such be true, then Brad and Janet
need not fear danger, for all the outrages
men can do would yield no more harm
than a picture of the stripèd tiger
to a man of flesh and bone.
However, inasmuch as our senses do tell,
we are all so much flesh and bone,
fated to feel and suffer in due season.
Tickle us, do we not laugh?
Prick us, do we not bleed?

GENTLEWOMAN
Weary us, do we not sleep?

THE BARD
Create a living homunculus and take it
to the seclusion of a somber bridal suite,
do we not feel apprehension and unease?

Exit THE BARD.

222 **trundle-bed:** a small bed, usually a pull-out

A Trundle-Bed.

223 **taper:** a long candle

224 **a score of seconds:** twenty seconds

SCENE 3. – *A Corridor in the Castle.*
Two upper Chambers can be seen, one occupied by JANET,
the other by BRAD.
ROCKY lies upon a Trundle-bed, bound with a Chain,
between them, and on a lower Level,
made as a portion of the Cell.

GROUNDLING
Janet's getting some practice,
grasping that candle...

JANET
This taper's light is feebly cast.
Methinks this guest-chamber hath the gloom
of a barred cell.

Enter FRANK, disguised as BRAD.
He enters Janet's Chamber.

JANET
Who goes there?

FRANK [*in BRAD'S voice*]
'Tis I, Brad. Come, Janet,
we have but one minute to love.

GENTLEMAN
I think he'll not endure
for a score of seconds!

JANET
Then draw nearer. But be thou silent,
lest others hear.

225 **aright:** correctly

226 **dandle:** play with

227 **guise:** disguise

228 **naught:** nothing

229 **urchin boy:** mischievous, ill-mannered boy

An Urchin.

230 **fruit:** You figure it out. You gotta learn sometime.

Fruit.

FRANK [*in BRAD'S voice*]
Mark them not! They know us not.
What care they what we do, or we what they think?

JANET
I pray thou speak'st aright.
Come, that I may dandle thy hair.
'Zounds! You are not Brad!

FRANK [*as himself*]
E'en in this poor light, thou hast seen through my guise.
Nonetheless, am I not pleasing?

JANET
O monstrous! Thou beast! What have you done with Brad?

FRANK
I have done naught with him.
Wherefore thy concern? Think you,
perhaps, I should have taken some liberty?

JANET
You speak of liberties! What of the deceit
you have play'd upon my person?
Like some urchin boy in the meadow
you pluck'd the fruit I reserved for my lord.

FRANK
Aye, I did. To that I admit.
Yet, confess, it pleased you as much
to give your fruit as it pleased me to eat of it.

> GROUNDLING
> Wait, I'm lost. Are they arguing
> because he *ate* something?

231 **privily:** in private

232 **O curb thy tongue!:** Oh, shut up!

GENTLEMAN
'Tis metaphor. I will explain it to you
privily, after the play.

JANET
O curb thy tongue! Brad! Help! O Brad!

FRANK
Hush! You'll disturb his rest. Besides,
to see you like this would give him unease.

JANET
Do not pretend that I am the blameworthy one!
This misdeed is your doing, and yours alone!
For my whole life, I had been saving myself.

FRANK
Verily, thou hast saved.
But thou art not yet full spent!

GENTLEMAN
Methinks the lady doth protest too much!

JANET
O, I am twice ruined!
Prithee, say naught to Brad of this.

FRANK
Thy secret is safe.

*FRANK leaves Janet's Chamber
and disguises himself as JANET,
pausing midway between the Chambers.*

*Enter RIFF-RAFF and MAGENTA, with Brooms and Mops,
onto the lower Level.*

233 **vex yourself:** worry yourself

234 **Neptune:** ancient Roman god of the sea

235 **pall:** gloom; sense of dread

236 **domestics:** household servants in a castle

237 **onerous:** unpleasant

238 **ammonium:** ammonia

239 **poor 'pothecary:** An apothecary, as you might recall from *Romeo and Juliet*, is a pharmacist. In Shakespeare's day, an apothecary, being a chemist of sorts, might provide a number of different chemicals, medicinal, marginally medicinal, and completely otherwise.

240 **effervescence:** fizz, usually the reaction of a base, such as sodium bicarbonate (baking soda) in an acid, such as vinegar

241 **flags:** flagstones; large pieces of slate or shale used as floor tiles

MAGENTA
Out! Out, damnèd spot!

RIFF-RAFF
Sister, vex yourself not more than is meet to do,
for such stains as this, all Neptune's
great ocean may not wash away.
Dr. Faustus hath wrought a deed that he cannot undo,
when he poor Edward Cutlet
did in scarlet passion slay.

MAGENTA
Verily, 'tis true.
He hath brought this pall 'pon us all,
by his own hand, and with no help of us.
Were we not playing the role of domestics here,
no kneeling and scrubbing would we do
to cleanse away the blood he had spilt this night.

RIFF-RAFF
Aye, none at all.

MAGENTA
Yet still, this task would less onerous be
had we but a bottle of ammonium,
such as a poor 'pothecary
might procure for a penny.

RIFF-RAFF
Indeed, I know exactly the kind!
Infused therein with effervescence,
that act as scrub-brushes 'pon these flags.
Aye, scrubbing bubbles. By their alchemy
one may do the job with half the toil, in half the time,
and with better outcome than with pond-water alone.

242 **broadsheet:** large printed notice, such as an advertisement

243 **leonine:** lion-like

244 **asunder:** apart

The task done, this castle floor agleam,
one stands triumphant, as Master Clean!

> GROUNDLING
> What is this, a broadsheet?

> GENTLEMAN
> In a manner of speaking.
> 'Tis the placement of product
> within the play. It helps keep
> the price of admission down,
> that persons of your standing,
> or lack thereof, may attend.

MAGENTA
Aye, aye, Master Clean.
Yet I scour this blood again.
Out! Out, damnèd spot!

ROCKY moves upon the Trundle-bed.

RIFF-RAFF
Speaking of Spots, mark now the master's new pet.
How he skulks like a guilty child.
Or, rather, like one afear'd.
Behold his brawny sinews leonine!
Yet he cowers like a kitten from his very shadow.

MAGENTA
He knoweth not his own strength,
else he would tear you asunder for your note.

> GROUNDLING
> Now Riff-Raff's grabbing a candle!
> Everyone's growing frisky!

245 **thrice:** three times

246 **toilet:** Again, not what you think. In this case, it means his quick makeup change.

RIFF-RAFF
A taper! Aflame, I shall brand 'pon his puny brain, -
his clay brain - wisdom enough to fear me!
Ha! Rocky, thou pebble! Thou clod of earth!
Thou Prometheus in form only, who pisses himself
and flies from my fire when I shake it in thy face!
Avaunt!

> *ROCKY breaks his Chain and makes to flee.*
> *RIFF-RAFF pursues ROCKY.*
> *ROCKY escapes down a Shaft in the floor.*

RIFF-RAFF
Take heed, Rocky, for 'tis tombish dark down there!
Here is a candle to light you to bed!

> *ROCKY cries out as if burnt.*

MAGENTA
Brother, was such cruelty warranted?

RIFF-RAFF
Come, now, thou didst enjoy my sport.
Let us now touch elbows thrice, in the manner of our land,
for I sense our victory to be drawing near at hand.

> GROUNDLING
> A couch of incest is the best,
> put your sister to the test.

> *Exeunt RIFF-RAFF and MAGENTA.*
> *FRANK completes his toilet*
> *and enters Brad's Chamber.*

247 **bastion:** a strong, sturdy structure

FRANK [*in JANET'S voice*]
O Brad, my lord, we must flee this place!
Doctor Faustus means to destroy us.

BRAD
Be not afear'd, Janet. Do but draw close
and lay with me awhile. Come dawn
we shall rise with the lark and depart
with the dew.

FRANK [*in Janet's voice*]
O Brad, a bastion of strength thou art,
and protective besides.

GROUNDLING
Haw! She just called him a bastard!

BRAD
Come, that I may dandle thy hair.

GENTLEMAN
...Dandle thy candle!

BRAD
'Zounds! You are not Janet!

GROUNDLING
She's a he!

FRANK [*as himself*]
E'en in this poor light, thou hast seen through my guise.
Nonetheless, am I not pleasing?

BRAD
O monstrous! Thou beast! What have you done with Janet?

248 **low'ring:** lowering; descending

249 **feign:** fake, as in "She's faking it."

250 **chicanery:** trickery

251 **Desist!:** Stop!

252 **Hist!:** Shh!

FRANK
I have done naught with her. Why?
Think you I ought?

BRAD
O treachery! Lies, and deceit!
Never, nevemever…
Never would I –

FRANK
O rest thy weary tongue!

GENTLEWOMAN
But he's only begun
to ready it for the chase!

FRANK
'Tis not all bad.
Not by half. Methinks thou didst rather enjoy it.
Thy low'ring scepter was at full mast,
and while a woman might feign delight,
a man hath not means for such chicanery.
If his staff be upraised, then so be his blood!

GENTLEMAN
Unless, in troth, he be only
grasping a candle!

BRAD
Desist! Oh, Janet! I am fortune's fool!

FRANK
Hist! Janet may be sleeping near.
Wish you her to come hither,
Bearing candle, only to cast light 'pon this?

253 **base-born knave:** oaf of common blood

254 **ire:** anger; fury

255 **reward … gauntlet:** slap you with the back of my glove – the customary challenge to a duel

256 **set our cocks a-crow … merry tune sing:** a typically Shakespearean pun that would have cracked 'em up back in the day, but is quite lost on modern ears. "Cock" is a word for rooster, the male chicken, which as you might know is wont to crow loudly in the morning. The lark is a songbird, more melodious of note, also partial to singing at sunup. "Cock" also meant then what it means now, or close to it, which should allow you to put the whole sordid picture together in your dirty little head.

257 **pique:** arouse

258 **deflower'd:** deflowered; relieved of one's virginity

BRAD
Cast not your share of blame upon me!
You know that all fault lies entirely with you.
You tricked me, you base-born knave...

FRANK
Base-born! Were you not so amusing in your ire,
I'd reward you with the back of my gauntlet.
In truth, confess, thou didst enjoy it.

GROUNDLING
Thank you, sir, may I have another?

FRANK
In giving oneself o'er to pleasure,
there is no crime. Come, let us
set our cocks a-crow
ere the lark his merry tune sing!
As for Janet, I shall sing not one note.
The delights we savor need not
pique her appetites.

GROUNDLING
Whoa... This is getting pretty gay now...

BRAD
I admit, it was pleasing,
to be touched in such manner, I do confess.
Once more unto the breach – but do swear
you will never breathe a word on this matter.

GENTLEMAN
O Frank! Do tell us
where you were deflower'd!

259 **abscond:** escape

260 **privy:** bathroom. At the time, this consisted (in a castle or city house) of a small room built into an outer wall. There was a seat with a hole cut into it opening up into a cesspool – an open pit full of rainwater, mud, and of course, bodily waste. A curious additional fact: many privies had a space to one side, called the garderobe, fitted with a closet bar for hanging one's finer clothing. Only the very plainest clothing, worn by peasants, could stand washing; anything more fashionable would be quickly ruined or fall apart. The pungent ammonia fumes wafting up from the cesspool, it was discovered, kept bugs from setting up shop in the clothing and eating it. It was rather like packing clothes in mothballs nowadays. I assume the clothes were given a good shake before wearing, to air them out a bit.

FRANK
By my troth, upon my mother's grave, I do swear.

Enter RIFF-RAFF.

RIFF-RAFF
My lord, your playmate he has burst his bond
and taken flight. He did abscond
and runs within the castle grounds.
Magenta has released the hounds.

FRANK
My Rocky? O! I come!

                                    GROUNDLING
                                    Not until Brad does!

*GENTLEMAN gives his hand to GROUNDLING
in the manner known in the Western Colonies
as a "High-Five".
GENTLEWOMAN is mortified.
Exeunt FRANK and RIFF-RAFF.*

JANET [*awakening*]
O spite! O hell!
I know not what is happening!
Whither Brad? Whither anyone?

                                    GENTLEWOMAN
                                    Whither the privy?

JANET
I pace the floor like a cagèd beast.
I know not where Brad has been quartered.
But look, the philosopher's cell.

261 **fallen:** ended up

262 **rampallions:** crazy people

263 **Magus:** magician, specifically of the Zoroastrian faith

264 **ken:** ability to see

265 **are wont to:** prefer to

Mayhap it will be conducive to my thought
as it was to Dr. Frank N. Furter's.

JANET descends to the Cell.

O Brad, fairest Brad!
I am to blame for this misfortune.
O, had we not set out upon this journey!
O, if only thy carriage had not lost a wheel!
If only we had fallen amongst friends,
or at least sane persons,
not these moon-mad rampallions.
But this morn I was yet a maid,
that ne'er before invited eyes,
tho' I had been gaz'd on like a comet.
Now of a sudden I am become a fallen star;
once having tasted base Earth,
never again to know the pure firmament.
What's this? A seeing-crystal?
Of such things I have heard.
The Magus of Persia's golden sands
doth use suchwise to espy lands
and people far beyond the ken
of his eyes alone.
Perhaps it shall reveal to me
Brad's whereabouts. O glassy orb!
Shew to me my lord Brad!
Behold – as the storm-clouds' cloak
doth part before the lancing beams of Helios,
so doth this crystal's darkness yield
an image, clear as...
... well, crystal. Sorry.
What, ho! 'Tis Brad,
but in his hand a pipe of clay,
such as men are wont to smoke when passion's spent!

266 **hob-nail:** nail used to attach a sole to a shoe

267 **possessed of:** possessing

268 **fustian:** fickle; faithless

A Fool.

269 **dross:** stuff; clutter

270 **poultice:** a compress used to soothe an injury or draw out a poison

271 **ell:** an old English unit of length equal to about 1.14 meter, or 45 inches, something like an ancient cubit. It was customarily used for measuring out cloth.

And beside him – a wig! A vile rug
that doth my hair resemble
as does a tarnished hob nail head
resemble the moon! O false man!
Verily, this is the work of Faustus –
But he could not have so pressed his will upon Brad
had Brad not been willing.
Brad is a man, possessed of a man's strength,
and could have cast the doctor off like an ill-cut coat
had he the will to do so.
O Brad! Thou fickle, fustian,
faithless fool!

Enter ROCKY.

JANET
Rocky? But thou'rt hurt!
Who hath done this thing to you?
A bite, as from a dog of war,
or a hound bred out of the Spartan kind!
Among this dross there must be
bandages, stuff of which to make a poultice,
that I may dress thy wounds.
None, I see none. The hem
of my chemise must serve to bind them.

JANET tears her garment to make a Bandage.

GROUNDLING
That won't be enough, Janet.
Tear off another ell, at the very least!

*Enter THE BARD, opposed, and MAGENTA and COLUMBIA,
bearing a Seeing-Crystal.*

272 **liver:** It was believed that the liver was the seat of emotions, particularly love.

273 **moon-beams:** It was also believed that the Moon could cause madness. ("Lunatic" means "made mad by the Moon".)

274 **chaste:** pure; innocent

THE BARD
Emotion, such as of a troubled liver,
or agitation upon the mind, as of moon-beams...
of such seething brain was Lady Janet.
It did act upon her as master,
powerful and irrational tyrant.
Magenta and Columbia did espy,
through a seeing-crystal of their own,
Janet and Rocky in the Cell,
and little doubt they held
that Janet was, indeed, its slave.

Exit THE BARD.

MAGENTA
The Magus of Persia's golden sands
doth use suchwise to espy lands
and people far beyond the ken
of his eyes alone.

                                    GENTLEMAN
                    We've heard this refrain!
                        Come, a song!

MAGENTA and COLUMBIA
Relate to us your tale of stolen love, O Janet!

JANET [*Sings.*]
    I'd lie a-night, the bed-sheets tight
    between my fingers, my knuckles white.
    Only the most chaste kisses had I known.

COLUMBIA
A maiden, then, she was?

275 **unmarred:** unmarked; undamaged

276 **battlements:** the protective outer walls of a castle or fortress. Like bulwarks and bastions. Something about the letter "B"...

277 **slaked:** quenched; satisfied

278 **stoked:** roused up; fired up

279 **peascod:** pea-pod

Gath'ring a Peascod.

280 **tilling:** plowing

MAGENTA
Aye, a most maidenly maiden, and chaste.

GROUNDLING
Chased all over the place!

JANET
> *Upon my virtue I posted guard,*
> *my heart behind a window barred.*
> *Though Brad I lov'd, I stayed unmarred.*
> *But now my battlements they are broke,*
> *and I have found my humors woke.*
> *Not slaked, my appetite be stoked.*

MAGENTA and COLUMBIA
Pray, tell us more!

JANET
> *My bulwarks they hath fallen in*
> *and become open gates for sin.*
> *Desire seizes now my limbs –*
> *I need a rugged man therein.*
>
> *Touch me now, O rugged man!*
> *Touch me with thy gentle hand.*
> *Touch me now, I do command!*
> *Creature of the night.*
>
> *Should your peascod ripen'd be*
> *while you're busy tilling me,*
> *I'll gather it most merrily*
> *and eat its peas, and cast it down.*

MAGENTA and COLUMBIA [*Sing.*]
> *Down, derry-derry-derry-down down.*

JANET

> *The idle hours I'd while away*
> *gath'ring peascods whilst I may.*
> *Take me for thy sport and play;*
> *all that thou art I'll make mine own.*
>
> *And that is but one taste of bread*
> *compared to what I have not said.*
> *Come, to a bedchamber we will tread*
> *and plant 'til ev'ry seed is sown!*
>
> *Touch me now, O rugged man!*
> *Touch me with thy gentle hand.*
> *Touch me now, I do command!*
> *Creature of the night.*

COLUMBIA

> *Touch me now, O rugged man!*

MAGENTA

> *Touch me with thy gentle hand.*

COLUMBIA

> *Touch me now, I do command!*

MAGENTA

> *Creature of the night.*

JANET

> *Touch me now, O rugged man!*
> *Touch me with thy gentle hand.*
> *Touch me now, I do command!*
> *Creature of the night.*

ROCKY

> *Creature of the night.*

281 **hatchling:** newborn

282 **bound fast:** tied or chained tightly

JANET
>*Creature of the night.*

ROCKY
>*Creature of the night.*

ALL
>*Creature of the night.*

>*Exeunt omnes. Enter FRANK, RIFF-RAFF and BRAD.*
>*FRANK is beating RIFF-RAFF.*

RIFF-RAFF
Mercy! Have mercy, O master!

FRANK
Poisonous bunch-back'd toad!
How came this to happen?

>   GROUNDLING
>   Beats me, but I have a hunch!

FRANK
I posted you on watch.
Now my hatchling has flown. The fault lies with thee!

RIFF-RAFF
Marry, I was distracted but one minute... master.
Chained he was to his trundle-bed, bound fast.

FRANK
Here is a seeing-crystal.
The Magus of Persia's golden sands
doth use suchwise to espy lands
and people far beyond the ken
of his eyes alone.

283 **knurl:** something bent or deformed

284 **threescore:** sixty

285 **hoary:** not what you think. It means "gray".

286 **denizen:** inhabitant

GENTLEWOMAN
Heard we not this before?

GENTLEMAN
Twice already.

FRANK
Gaze ye into its glassy deeps
and seek out my Rocky. Go!
Here is the back of my hand, bent knurl!
Perhaps more beatings about the face
may improve thy vision!

RIFF-RAFF
My lord, I see not Rocky, but a visitor.
A man of some threescore years, hoary of head...

GROUNDLING
Haw! He said "hoary"!

RIFF-RAFF
...In a wheeled chair.

BRAD
A wheeled chair? Let me peer therein.
'Zounds! 'Tis no less than Doctor Everett of Scotland.

RIFF-RAFF
You are acquainted with this denizen of this poor globe?
... I mean to say, with this... man?

BRAD
Verily! Erstwhile professor of mine at university.
We scholars were fond of him, and would
call him "Scotty".

287 **design:** plan

288 **portents:** signs of things to come (Again with the astrology)

289 **wand'ring spheres:** planets

290 **trip:** to walk upon

GROUNDLING
Beam me up!

FRANK
I sense a deception here. You did not, then,
arrive at my castle by mere chance,
but with some design in mind.

BRAD
You do wrong me, sir. My carriage lost a wheel.
You have my word on that.

FRANK
So you have told me; aye, I have heard.
However, this Doctor Everett –
His name is not unknown to me.

BRAD
He was a professor of Philosophy at the University
at Denton, and of no little renown.

FRANK
More than a mere schoolteacher, methinks,
is he not, Brad? He is in the employ of the king,
and advises him regarding strange portents
in the heavens, disasters in the sun,
travelers from the wand'ring spheres,
worlds like this, yet alien and curious-wrought,
that track the far-flung orbits of distant stars.
Travelers to this world, who trip your very shores
with their foreign feet. These doth your Doctor Scott
make study of. Is that not so, Brad?

BRAD
This may be so, yet such conceits
seem more fable and fancy to me than Philosophy.

291 **Sativa:** Not actually a Hindu goddess (although there's a professional dominatrix in Los Angeles who goes by the name Goddess Sativa). *Cannabis sativa* is the scientific name for one of the specie of hemp, or marijuana plant.

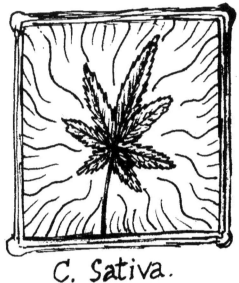

C. Sativa.

292 **labyrinth:** maze

293 **Ariadne:** in Greek mythology, the daughter of King Minos of Crete. She gave the hero Theseus a ball of string to unwind behind him so he could find his way back out of the labyrinth beneath her father's castle.

He is a scholar, and his passions
are many. I do not know.

FRANK
Fable and fancy? Perhaps 'tis as well
you regard them as suchlike,
and no more.

RIFF-RAFF
He intrudes, master. He has entered the castle,
though I did lock the gates.

FRANK
Though legless, he hath by magic o'erstepped
my threshold. But he is now in my domain,
and here my magic holds greater power.
He hath entered unto my chamber of meditation,
a cloister'd closet wherein, in the spicèd Indian air
sacred to the goddess Sativa, one may pursue
the extinction of one's self, and by extension
all desires and resulting sorrows.
One might dine on lotus-leaves,
and regard life and death as all alike.

BRAD
Knowest thou this tranquility of spirit?

FRANK
Look I tranquil to you?
Mark my words, I now draw him in
like a fish, thro' the labyrinth of my castle,
as though hook'd on Ariadne's thread.
I steer him 'round and 'round the bed
where Magenta and Columbia pillow their head –
Weave a circle 'round them thrice,
and close your eyes in holy dread!

294 **roughcast:** a plaster of quicklime, cement, and gravel, used on outside walls

295 **henceforth:** from here on

296 **marbled:** multicolored

The Marbled Serpent.

See, Riff-Raff! See, Brad! I reel him in.
Now in the kitchen, now the great hall,
now in the privy, most foul of stall.
now in the grand room where we all have a ball,
now crash like mortar-shell through solid stone wall!

> *Enter DR. EVERETT the SCOT, in Wheeled Chair,*
> *through a Wall, of loam and roughcast made.*

BRAD
Great Scot!

> *GROUNDLING roughly casts a Roll of Privy Paper.*

EVERETT
Damnèd roughcast...
Faustus Frank N. Furter, we meet at last.

BRAD
Doctor Everett!

EVERETT
Lord Brad! Wherefore art thou here, in this den of iniquity?

FRANK
Play not the fool, Doctor Everett. Knowest you well
Brad Majors' purpose here.
Wishing to know my designs,
which I kept well hid from you,
you did send him, and his lady companion,
to act as spies, under guise of simple
lost travelers. Forsooth!
No matter; henceforth,
I alter my plans, changing them
as the marbled serpent trades his skin
for new when worn out.

297 **behooves:** benefits

298 **cast augurs:** do fortunetelling

It behooves one to be so adaptable,
Doctor Everett. I know full well
that Brad is.

GENTLEMAN
Brad's pendulum doth swing both ways!

EVERETT
Nay, Faustus. Brad's presence here
I did not anticipate.
'Tis Edward Cutlet I seek, no more.

BRAD
This Edward did I see this eventide.

FRANK
You speak of Edward! What know you of Edward,
Doctor Everett?

EVERETT
Much do I know, O Faustus, about a great many things.
But regarding Edward, I need not consult my books,
nor cast augurs. Young Edward is my nephew,
as happenstance might have it.

BRAD
O grim day! O heavy deed!
Doctor Everett...

Enter JANET and ROCKY, all of a hurry.

JANET
Ah!

EVERETT
Lady Janet!

299 **Bullwinkle:** an obscure reference to a literary or folkloric character well-known in Shakespeare's day, whose significance is currently lost to us.

300 **Adrienne:** like the aforementioned Bullwinkle, another obscure reference to a literary or folkloric character well-known in Shakespeare's day, whose significance is currently lost to us.

301 **selfsame:** the very same

JANET
Doctor Everett the Scot!

BRAD
Janet!

JANET
My lord!

FRANK
Rocky!

                                             GROUNDLING
                                               Bullwinkle!

EVERETT
Lady Janet!

JANET
Doctor Everett!

BRAD
Janet!

JANET
My lord!

FRANK
Rocky!

                                             GROUNDLING
                        Adrienne! I did it for you!

FRANK
Mark my words, Rocky. I made thee,
and I can unmake thee with selfsame effort.

302 **spurn:** disregard

Enter MAGENTA, sounding a Gong.

MAGENTA
Master, dinner is prepared.

FRANK
Excellent. All here are welcome,
as I want not for victuals.
Under the circumstances, we
shall come attired as we are,
spurning formal dress.
The activities of this evening hath
kindled in me an appetite most voracious.

Exeunt omnes together.

Doctor Everett
& Scot.

SCENE 4. – *A Dining-Hall.*

Enter RIFF-RAFF and MAGENTA,
who set forth the silver.
Enter THE BARD, opposed.

THE BARD
In all of Life's rituals, food has always played
a role, vital and central.
The breaking of bread, the last meal
of the condemned man...

                                    GENTLEWOMAN
              Pray, wherefore seven forks at one setting?

THE BARD [*to Magenta*]
Indeed, wherefore such a mob of forks?

MAGENTA
Doctor Everett is in a wheeled chair.
Should he drop a fork, he need not pick it up.

THE BARD
How long hast thou been a domestic?
Should a guest drop a utensil, a servant
need only pass him a clean one. 'Tis thy duty.

MAGENTA
Our lord feels that this way is far more insulting.

RIFF-RAFF
It seems considerate, but in a way
that calls attention to his handicap.

303 **bon-ami:** camaraderie

304 **short shrift:** peremptory treatment

305 **shift:** chemise

306 **salver:** a large platter

307 **slighted:** insulted; ignored

308 **Timon of Athens:** subject of another drama of Shakespeare's. Timon was so generous that he went broke, at which point his friends abandoned him. To shame them, he invited them to a banquet that turned out to be bowls of warm water.

309 **Titus Andronicus:** subject of another play, mentioned earlier in this book. He, too, hosts a banquet. How to put this delicately? Four of his enemies are there, but he only needs chairs for two of them. Plates suffice for the other two.

310 **make your gorge rise:** I think I just threw up a little.

THE BARD
Forsooth!
It would appear that this meal,
although informal of dress,
will give the *bon-ami* of friends short shrift indeed.

GENTLEWOMAN
Short shrift, as befits
Lady Janet's short shift.

Exit THE BARD.
Enter FRANK, COLUMBIA, BRAD, JANET,
ROCKY and DR. EVERETT.
All take their seats. MAGENTA and RIFF-RAFF
bring forth the meat upon a covered Salver.
They serve it, and pour the wine.

GENTLEWOMAN
Such quantity of steam issues from 'neath that lid!
Will this be a droll feast of warm water,
like unto the one slighted Timon of Athens
did serve his false friends in that other play we saw?

GENTLEMAN
Er... Methinks this repast is more like
the one in the *other* play we saw last year,
about Titus Andronicus.
The one you likèd not, and that
did make your gorge rise to think 'pon it.
It giveth new meaning to
"What a number of men eat Timon,
and Timon sees it not."

GENTLEWOMAN
O men! What means this preoccupation
with such unseemliness?

311 **contrivance:** device; contraption; utensil

GENTLEMAN
'Tis but a play.

FRANK
O Rocky, forbear to eat
until all have been served, and I
hath given indication to begin.

COLUMBIA
Aye, and do use this contrivance, Rocky.
'Tis called a fork.

GROUNDLING
Hey, Edward! Get your arse off the table!

FRANK
The meat hath been carved, the cups hath been filled.
A toast, then, to absent friends.

ALL
To absent friends.

FRANK
And to Rocky besides.
[*Sings.*]
> To me, fair friend, you never can be old,
> for as you were when first your eye I ey'd,
> such seems your beauty still.
> With a fa-la-la-la-la, and a hey, nonny-nonny...

JANET [*Sings.*]
> With a fa-la-la-la-la, and a hey, nonny-nonny...

FRANK
I was not born under a singing planet.
Shall we now eat?

312 **haggis:** a fabled Scottish delicacy, a sort of sausage or thick pudding made of sheep or calf offal (minced organ meats) mixed with suet (fat), oatmeal and spices, and boiled in a bag traditionally made from the animal's stomach, nowadays an artificial edible casing. Despite what it sounds like, I've heard it's not bad at all.

313 **depredations:** bad behavior

314 **wastrels:** scoundrels, but lacking the patina of rogueish romanticism that Han Solo found so appealing.

EVERETT
Although this meat is much improv'd
over my usual haggis,
I came to your castle to discuss Edward.
Where is my nephew?

COLUMBIA
Edward? Your nephew?

FRANK
That is a subject most tender.
By the way, there are cutlets in plenty.
Should anyone care for another pound
of flesh, he need only ask.

COLUMBIA [*Screams.*]
Oh! I beg forgiveness of this company.
I am of a sudden taken ill.

Exit COLUMBIA, screaming.

GROUNDLING
She thought the meat tasted
a little too familiar.

EVERETT
My nephew, Doctor Faustus, young Edward.
I confess that, although I lov'd him like a son,
I could no more govern his wills
than his parents could.
Yet he did take care to send me a message
some few days ago, that gave me concern
that his misadventures and depredations
had taken a turn so dark as to frighten even him.
I knew he had fallen in with scoundrels and wastrels,
but I see now that his company included

315 **Anthropophagi**: cannibals, from Greek ανθρωποφάγοι *Anthropos* = men + *phagi* = eaters of. The character Calaban in Shakespeare's last play, *The Tempest*, is believed to be a cannibal, although he does not devour anyone on-stage or off-, because his name is an anagram of "canabal". The one-eyed, one-horned, flying purple people eaters, reported by the European explorer Shelby Wooley circa 1958, are often mistakenly assumed to eat human flesh; however, further research indicates that this is limited only to purple people and that the beasts are otherwise of a gentle disposition.

316 **men whose heads ... shoulders:** Doctor Everett lists but two of many monstrous beings travelers reported as living in faraway lands. It is thought that they might in fact have been gorillas or orangutans, who are man-like in general form but whose heads are positioned lower.

Men whose heads
do grow beneath
their shoulders.

317 **would seem but commonplace beside:** Compared to Frank & Co., such monsters would seem ordinary.

318 **many a merry bottle crack'd we together:** Wittenburg U. still stands today as a center of higher learning. As their official transcripts, kept on file in the Permanent Records dungeon, substantiate, it seems that Doctor Everett and Hamlet wasted a semester drinking a lot.

men of such strange origin...
The Cannibals that each other eat,
the *Anthropophagi*; and men whose heads
do grow beneath their shoulders – these and more
would seem but commonplace
beside those whose company young Edward
now kept. Yea, he dwelt with beasts
in men's form, but from lands so distant
as to be from off this Earth. Aye,
travelers from another star.

ROCKY
I am slow of study, and comprehendeth not.

BRAD
Doctor Everett! What meanest thou?

FRANK
Go on, Doctor Everett the Scot. Or should I say,
Doktor Everett van Helsing?

BRAD
Doctor Frank N. Furter! What meanest thou?

EVERETT
No doubt he speaks of my accent.
As a student myself, I attended University
at Wittenburg. Hamlet, Prince of Denmark,
my room-mate was, and many a merry bottle
crack'd we together of a week-end night!
Sadly, 'twas not to last. He did receive word
that his father, a Dane also by name of Hamlet,
had of a sudden passed of an illness,
and he did hie himself back to Denmark forthwith.
When he did not return, our Master had
no recourse but to mark him as a failure for

319 **hie:** hurry

320 **forthwith:** immediately

321 **I did receive ... my sheepskin:** a reference to a campus superstition that if one's college roommate dies, the surviving roommate receives an automatic 4.0 GPA for the semester as compensation. Don't believe it. All you'll get is counseling and a new roommate. The "sheepskin" refers to the diploma, after the parchment upon which it was printed.

322 **undescried:** undiscovered

323 **esculent:** substantial (also, fit to be eaten)

the semester. When later, we received
news of the prince's own death,
I did receive a commendation, out of pity's sake.
and thus did I earn my sheepskin.

BRAD
All a tale well-told... But what of thy accent?

GENTLEMAN
Aye! Speak ye plain and
to the point this time!

EVERETT
Wittenburg University is in German lands.
Being there did color my accent.

BRAD
Oh.

FRANK
Enough! Van Helsing is thy father's name.
Thou'rt not a Scot. Furthermore,
you make a study of things
best left undescried.

EVERETT
It is just as well!

BRAD
Doctor Everett! What meanest thou?

EVERETT
It is just as well, Lord Brad!
As I await more esculent news as regards
my absent nephew, I shall tell you
his sad tale in song.

324 **squandered most rankly:** wasted foolishly

325 **lewd catch-songs:** naughty songs, usually short, with a
double-entendre for a punch-line

Adam catch'd Eve
by ẙ Fur belowe —
And that's ẙ oldeſt
Catch I knowe.

A lewd catch-song.

Enter THE BARD, unseen.

EVERETT [*Sings.*]
Truly, Edward was born – in an hour of weeping,
for never a child – was of more woe.

GROUNDLING
Woe, woe, woe...

EVERETT
And his mother's sweet care...

THE BARD
He repaid with unending despair.

EVERETT
And when she died, he did go.
His inheritance squandered most rankly –
lewd catch-songs and whores, a fleet-footed steed.
His love for drink was immense.

GROUNDLING
Glug – *BURRRP!!!*

THE BARD
Methinks he was a general offence!

GENTLEWOMAN
As was that report you gave!

GROUNDLING
Thank you! I thought it was superb.

EVERETT
His companions he'd mislead.

326 **churl:** an oaf

327 **creep:** a jerk. Interestingly, the earliest extant printed use of "creep" as a noun meaning "a loathsome person" dates back *almost* as far as Shakespeare. Close enough for me!

328 **Verily:** In truth

329 **Wax ye not ... noise!:** Don't grow angry at their talk.

330 **mangy cur:** a dog with hair falling out

331 **canker-sore:** a painful sore in the mouth or mucous membranes. Take your vitamins and brush twice daily.

332 **half-dram:** about 1.5 mL, or 1/16 of a fluid ounce

333 **ink and quill:** before text messaging...

Ink & quill.

ALL
> *When Edward kept away while other children played,*
> *a base-born churl you knew he'd be.*
> *But when he held forth his sword 'gainst his own sworn*
> *blood...*

FRANK
> *What a creep!*

JANET
> *Makes one weep.*

EVERETT
> *Verily.*

> *Enter COLUMBIA, unseen.*

COLUMBIA *[To the tune of "Early One Morning"]*
> *Although to Milord I stayed true, I was drawn to Edward*
> *too.*
> *The more the scorn that he did earn, the more did my love*
> *grow.*
> *I bade him, hearken to my voice: Wax ye not wroth unto*
> *their noise!*
> *But he closed his ears and shut me out and saddened my*
> *heart so.*

> *Exit COLUMBIA.*

EVERETT *[Bringing forth a missive.]*
> *A mangy cur he was, indeed, a canker-sore; yet still,*
> *a half-dram of civility made him pick up ink and quill,*
> *and pen a note whose spelling is worse than any I've seen*
> *in class:*

334 **"*O hayste … com to pas!*"**: The joke here is that Edward's badly-scrawled letter is actually a reasonable approximation of Middle English – the language of Geoffrey Chaucer, author of The *Canterbury Tales*. Written in modern English, it reads:

> *"O haste; my brains do boil!*
> *I may shuffle off this mortal coil!*
> *Their evil deeds must never come to pass!"*

"Shuffle off this mortal coil" is from *Hamlet*; it means "to die".

GROUNDLING
What's it say? What's it say?

EVERETT

"*O hayste, mi braynes boyle!*
Y wis schuffle of thys mortall coyle!
Ther yvel dedes must neuere com to pas!"

GENTLEWOMAN
Get thee to a grammarian, go!

ALL

When Edward kept away while other children played,
a base-born churl you knew he'd be.
But when he held forth his sword 'gainst his own sworn
blood...

FRANK

What a creep!

JANET

Makes one weep.

EVERETT

Verily.

ALL

When Edward kept away while other children played,
a base-born churl you knew he'd be.
But when he held forth his sword 'gainst his own sworn
blood...

FRANK

What a creep!

335 ***Miserere mei, Deus***: Latin for "Have mercy on me, O God."
   This is from a setting of Psalm 51 by Italian composer Gregorio
   Allegri, probably during the 1630s.

336 **strumpet:** a loose woman; a prostitute

ALL
Woe, and woe, O woe...

JANET
Makes one weep.

ALL
Miserere mei, Deus...

EVERETT
Verily.
[*Speaks.*] This letter, however badly writ,
deserves my attention, as Edward's uncle
and as a man of honor, and it is what drew
me to your castle – Not your magician's tricks!

                              GROUNDLING
                    Admit it – you came for the food!

EVERETT
I demand to know where stays my nephew.

FRANK
Very well. Edward Cutlet is close at hand.

FRANK lifts the cover from the Salver
fully, revealing EDWARD'S half-devoured Carcase.
All scream. JANET flies into ROCKY'S arms.

FRANK
Rocky, forsooth! A woman's charms are not for thee!
Get thee hence, thou strumpet! [*Strikes Janet.*]

RIFF-RAFF [*to Magenta, whose screams have to laughter turned*]
Curb thy tongue!

337 **ungovernable:** uncontrollable

338 **was wont to share his affections:** liked to share his affections

339 **sheep's guts ... bodies:** Sweet music sends us into heightened emotional states. (Sheep intestine was at one time used to make so-called "catgut" strings for instruments such as lutes and violins.)

FRANK
Poor Edward! I, too, had a fondness for him.
A fellow of infinite jest.
But he prov'd ungovernable, and was wont
to share his affections with others,
a freedom I could not permit.
Furthermore, he had grown soft.
Now, having Rocky, I took the last
of Edward, and sent him on his way.

FRANK covers the Salver.

JANET
How could you do something so inhuman?

FRANK
Inhuman? If you only knew!
There is more in Heaven and Earth, Janet,
than is dreamt of in your Philosophy.
[*Sings.*]
> *Now is the time to unbind thy mind –*
> *You had best grow wise, Janet Weiss.*
> *You've lived nineteen years, yet known naught but fears;*
> *your life you've not lived, Janet Weiss!*
> *I've giv'n thee a taste of what lies in wait.*
> *'Tis for you to take the next bite, Janet Weiss.*
> *Knowest that sheep's guts hale souls from men's bodies.*
> *Your strings are wound far too tight, Janet Weiss!*
> *(They're ripe for plucking!)*
> *Art thou yet afear'd? To heart take this advice:*
> *You had best grow wise, Janet Weiss.*
> *You had best grow wise.*

GROUNDLING
You'd best spread your thighs,
Janet Weiss!

340 **fixed:** attached; stuck

341 **by Jesu:** by Jesus. Maybe it was felt that dropping the "s" at the end made it less of a swear.

FRANK [*Speaks.*]
I hath further design for thee,
good company. First, I must hold you
fixed to the spot, as if by roots.

JANET
My feet! Would that I could fly!

GENTLEWOMAN
You'd best grow wings,
Janet Weiss!

EVERETT
My wheels! By Jesu, 'tis as though a beam
were thrust through their spokes!

GROUNDLING
Indeed, he's beamed you down, Scotty!

BRAD
It is as we had walked upon
warm wax, or tree tar,
and been trapped, insect-like, where we stand!

FRANK
My spell is took! Trapped you are.
with fear you quake in your boots,
yet are powerless to run!

GROUNDLING
State the obvious, Janet!

JANET
Friends, he means to trap us!

342 **firk:** to beat or strike

343 **Gorgon, Medusa:** In Greek mythology, the Gorgons were three beautiful sisters who offended the goddess Athena and were transformed into hideous monsters. Medusa, the most famous of the three, had serpents for hair, and one look into her eyes would turn one to stone.

A Gorgon.

344 **amethystine:** like amethyst, a greenish gemstone

345 **Cleopatra's Antony:** Julius Caesar's general Mark Antony was seduced by Cleopatra, Queen of Egypt. (Also subject of a play by Shakespeare.)

FRANK
Janet, waste not your substance
in pursuit of wind.

GENTLEMAN
I confess, I did father that one.

FRANK
In time thou wilt grow accustomed
to being my puppet, my slave.
You may in time even enjoy
how I do firk thy very mind!

GROUNDLING
Firk it but good!

FRANK
Magenta, bring hither my staff – the one
topp'd with silver Gorgon's head. Aye,
that's the one.
As Medusa, once so fair, now made monstrous,
turn'd to cold stone all who met her amethystine gaze...

GROUNDLING
...and lesbians...

FRANK
... so this staff hath power to render one petrified,
and as easily remove the heavy spell at my will.

EVERETT
Unlike Cleopatra's Antony,
we of this globe you won't find to be an easy mark.
No magic can sway the human heart,
even as it makes play with our bodies.

346 **transfix:** to petrify

347 **commit:** to force

348 **blow:** Not what you and the Groundling think. To send, as the blowing wind sends a ship.

I see that you have mastered that sorcery
which hath eluded philosophers:
the skill to transfix us so, and commit
our limbs to dance as you see fit.

BRAD
You mean to say...

EVERETT
Aye, Lord Brad. Many of learning have tried
this art, and failed complete. But it seems
our friend here hath met with success,
and indeed hath perfection attained.
Perfection, yes, and much more.
For this spell of conjuring, should my
memory serve, must give its master
powers well to send his subjects –
aye, us poor, frail subjects –
as little ships upon a vast ocean,
where he wills them, be it far afield,
to a distant star, or even to times past,
or to that undiscover'd country,
the unwritten future.

JANET
What meanest thou?
Hath he design to blow us
to a wand'ring planet?

GROUNDLING
I think he only blows men, Janet!

349 **foresworn:** lying: This statement, paraphrased from an observation made by Touchstone in *As You Like It*, boils down to "In matters of opinion, there are no wrong answers."

(It has little bearing on the song; but "mustard" only rhymes with "flustered" – a word that didn't exist until the 20th Century.)

350 **motley:** of varied colors, as a fool's garment

FRANK [*Sings.*]
>   *Planet? Pomegranate!*
>   *You had best grow wise, Janet Weiss.*
>   *You had best grow wise, and make great your thighs*
>   *by running, dancing, and... exercise.*
>   *You had best grow wise.*

>   *Enter THE BARD, unseen.*

THE BARD
And then she did cry out...

>   *Exit THE BARD.*

JANET
Stop, I pray thee!

FRANK
>   *A certain dame did swear by her honor*
>   *that the Frankfort sausage was good*
>   *and that the mustard was naught.*
>   *Now, I'll stand to it, the sausage was good,*

>   GENTLEMAN
>   I'll wager you found it so, Frank!

FRANK
>   *and the mustard was good as well,*
>   *and yet was not the dame foresworn.*

BRAD [*Sings.*]
>   *O motley fool thou'rt,*
>   *and a heat-mad dog besides!*
>   *But should you my lady hurt her,*
>   *I'll tear thee apart, O Frank N. Furter!*

351 **philanderer:** a guy who messes around with people other than his significant other

352 **doublet:** a vest-like garment, but considerably more fancy

353 **Saturn:** ancient Roman god/titan. Afraid that his offspring would overthrow him as he had usurped his own father Uranus, he took to devouring his children at birth.

Saturn.

354 **But to what avail?:** Fat lot of good it did me!

355 **a large naught ... a small one:** A big zero is the same as a small zero.

356 **twixt:** between

> FRANK directs Staff at BRAD,
> who becomes like unto a statue.

EVERETT [*Sings.*]
> O motley fool thou'rt,
> and a heat-mad dog besides!
> But should you that lady hurt her,
> I'll tear thee apart, O Frank N. Furter!

> > FRANK directs Staff at EVERETT,
> > who becomes like unto a statue.

JANET [*Sings.*]
> O motley fool thou'rt,
> and a heat-mad dog...

> > FRANK directs Staff at JANET,
> > who becomes like unto a statue.
> > Enter COLUMBIA.

COLUMBIA
O God! O Fate! No more can I bear!
Frank, thou faithless, fickle philanderer!
First thou did'st spurn me for Edward,
and then you cast him away like a worn doublet
for Rocky! Like cruel Saturn,
you devour people, yea, those people
whom you should love as thine own.
You chew them as the cow doth her clover
in her content, only to spit them out again.
I lovèd thee, mark my words, I did love thee!
But to what avail? A large naught is as much a naught
as a small one, so I say unto thee.
Like the sea-sponge, or a knob of bread
pinched twixt the fingers and dipped into wine,

357 **gluttony:** greed, one of the cardinal vices we'd all do well to avoid

358 **fabled Hellas:** storied Greece, referring to a long-ago Golden Age, when Art and Culture reigned supreme… (long before her current economic difficulties…)

you take what you will, the image of gluttony,
sucking others dry of their love, their emotion...

GROUNDLING
... their seed...

COLUMBIA
... and leave of them dry husks, bereft of feeling –
aye, all feeling, save that of regret,
of shame at having spent the best of themselves
on such as you! Enough; I can bear no more.
Make your choice, Frank. Wilt thou choose me,
Columbia, who hath been faithful unto thee
throughout thy dalliances – or Rocky, so named
for the quarry to be found between his ears?

FRANK
Caught 'twixt a rock and a hard place, indeed.

FRANK directs Staff at COLUMBIA,
who becomes like unto a statue.

FRANK
Ne'er had it been so difficult to enjoy
a pleasant time with good company.

FRANK directs Staff at ROCKY,
who becomes like unto a statue.

GROUNDLING
Great party! Now everyone's getting stoned!

FRANK
Now Rocky's marbled masses
do span his entire frame. O sculptors
of fabled Hellas, look upon my work with envy!

359 **How sharper than a serpent's tooth:** … it is to have a thankless child. (from *King Lear*, Act I, scene 4)

360 **recalcitrance:** reluctance

361 **pan:** brain-pan; where the brain sits in the skull

362 **metal:** There is a play on words here. He is using a broad, somewhat alchemical application of the word "metal" to refer to all solid geological matter, whether metal, metalloid, or mineral by today's definition. This is again a reference to the Judeo-Christian creation story in which the first man was made of clay. "Metal" also rhymes with "mettle", a term common in Shakespeare's time that meant "strength", either physical or personal.

363 **abed:** in bed

364 **impearl'd:** set like pearls or other gems

365 **mark:** to look for; to admire

My, but my face does ache to smile so,
when all my children do turn on me.
How sharper than a serpent's tooth,
and all that – Rocky's manner,
so rude and thankless,
doth bring to mind young Edward's
own recalcitrance at my attempts
to mold him to perfection.
I did draw half of Edward's brains
into the pan of Rocky's head.
Could that have been my error?
O would that I could make a man
of some other metal than earth!

RIFF-RAFF
Speaking, master, of Earth...

MAGENTA
O Faustus! Weary am I of this sphere!
When shall we return to Transylvania,
the stars from whence we came, and
for which we nightly yearn?
Each night abed I gaze upon them,
impearl'd upon the deep of the heavens,
and mark the stone that is my home,
where wait my own house, and my own bed,
and my own kinsmen.

FRANK
Magenta, I hear your pleas.
My gratitude to you, and to your brother,
Riff-Raff, is boundless, like the very heavens
'pon which you gaze nightly.
Well have you both served me, and I shall
be as generous tenfold in rewarding your loyalty.

366 **And you shall receive it... in abundance!:** a large naught

367 **masques:** masquerade ball

You will discover that I can be a most
beneficent master, when in a favorable mood.

MAGENTA
I ask for nothing... Master.

GROUNDLING
... bator.

FRANK
And you shall receive it... in abundance!

MAGENTA
So I thought.

FRANK
Come, now our masques are begun.
Come, now our revels commence!

Exit FRANK.

RIFF-RAFF
Let us again touch elbows thrice, in the manner of our land,
for I sense our victory to be drawing near at hand.

Exeunt MAGENTA and RIFF-RAFF.

Draw Curtain over scene.
Enter THE BARD.

THE BARD
O marvelous Fate! So the stars deemed
that Brad and Janet, though lost
and stray'd to Frank's castle, should yet keep
their appointment with Doctor Everett the Scot.

368 **pledging their troth:** getting engaged

369 **miscreant:** a no-good person

370 **persuasion:** unsavory proclivities

371 **outrages:** sins; transgressions

372 **machinations:** cunning plans

GENTLEMAN
The Scot who speaks like an Austrian?

THE BARD
Erm... Yes, that very same.
Yet although their planned
appointment was kept, 'twas in
a situation most unforeseen,
and beyond their imagining.
Within but mere hours of pledging their troth,
Brad and Janet had tasted of forbidden fruit,
and by Doctor Faustus' own hand.
Their host, it seems, was a miscreant
of questionable morals and some persuasion.
What further indignities,
what outrages of the flesh,
would yet be visited upon them this night?
And what of these masques, these revels,
performed to an empty house,
in the middle of the night...

GROUNDLING
Just like this play of yours!

THE BARD
What machinations perverse had seized
Doctor Faustus' fancies?

GENTLEMAN
The same that did seize some other part of him, methinks!

THE BARD
A touch, I do confess. Into that trap
heedless did I walk. But I proceed:

373 **poesy:** poetry

374 **fretted lute:** Any kid with a guitar knows this.

A Lute.

What plan indeed? If the traffic of our stage
of the past hour and half doth show
us what is to come, then we do know
that this orgy was to be no pleasant diversion,
such as a luncheon upon the greeny grass
along the banks of a brook,
where one might enjoy slices of cucumber
bedded 'twixt slices of bread,
and sip of Spanish wine, whilst
one's lady recites verses of poesy
from my book of Sonnets
(available for sixpence in the lobby)
to the time marked by one's manservant
upon the fretted lute...

GROUNDLING
You mean, a picnic?

THE BARD
No picnic!

Exit THE BARD.

GENTLEWOMAN
What, pray tell, is a "pic-nic"?

GENTLEMAN
Marry, I have not a clue,
save that it may be that pleasant
luncheon on the grass.

ACT III.

Scene 1. – *A large Chamber in* FRANK'S *Castle.*
Placed centrally is a large Basin, filled with water,
for bathing. Suspended above is a Mirror,
that the audience may see the bathers.

The Chamber opens, and discovers
COLUMBIA, ROCKY, BRAD, JANET and EVERETT,
yet like unto Statues,
now clothed to match FRANK.

Enter FRANK, bearing the Gorgon Staff.
He makes preparations for the revels,
lighting the tapers.

FRANK
Now I turn back the spell, one by one.
Musicians, run thy invisible fingers
upon the unseen strings of thy instruments.
Our revels now commence.

Music begins.
FRANK directs Staff at COLUMBIA,
who regains movement and dances.

COLUMBIA [*Sings.*]
> Full pleased was I when first to this castle came;
> I saw Frank through the lens of glorious fame.
> Nearly blind was I to his distracted game –
> his game to build a man to fan his flame!
> Now I clutch the tatters of his love,
> those tatters torn, for false that love did prove.

375 **Let me see only that pleaseth me:** Let me see only that which pleases me.

376 **matchless:** unequalled

377 **ravening:** severe; ravenous

378 **quell:** quench

Like spectacles of rosy glass,
let me see only that pleaseth me.

FRANK directs Staff at ROCKY,
who regains movement and dances.

ROCKY [*Sings.*]
But seven hours old am I, and know but naught.

GENTLEWOMAN
Thy dancing says as much!

ROCKY
Yet I am god-like, of matchless beauty wrought;
and it would be well that maids in school be taught
that I am the very man their parents liketh not.
I trust nothing save fleshly pleasure
which I mean to take in limitless measure.
Like spectacles of rosy glass,
let me see only that pleaseth me.

FRANK directs Staff at BRAD,
who regains movement and dances.

BRAD [*Sings.*]
This evening is a nightmare from which I cannot wake.
Like a babe who cries for Mother, I beg of thee to take
this dream away; I shall be good.
What, ho! These clothes that fit my form so well
do fill my veins with flickering fire.
Effulgent I am with lurid dancing desire.
Unsex me now! This ravening thirst I cannot quell!
With a hey, nonny-nonny and a bam'n-a-bip-bang.

379 **insensible:** unaware

380 **furl'd:** furled; rolled up

381 **fore:** the front, or foreground

382 **thews:** thighs

GENTLEWOMAN
The finest silken hose is wasted
on such knobbed twigs as his.

FRANK directs Staff at JANET,
who regains movement and dances.

JANET [*Sings.*]
My heart I'd always kept as bird in gilded cage,
of mine own sorrow insensible, knowing not my rage.
But 'pon this night, Frank did set me free.
What, ho! That cage can fit my heart no more.
Its wings, once furl'd, now span the world,
my mind hath the azure sky encircled!
Woman am I now! 'Tis Frank brought me to fore.
With a hey, nonny-nonny and a bam'n-a-bip-bang.

ALL
Like spectacles of rosy glass,
let me see only that pleaseth me.

A tucket of trumpets as a Tower is raised
over the Basin.

FRANK [*Sings.*]
A tragic tale did play, of Lady Wray,
favor'd beauty of bold King Kong, and how,
their lovers' stars were cross'd, love won and lost,
and thus was mighty monarch laid full low.
I did weep, as did we all that day –
but not for Kong, the tall and dark, expired.
Not for him, nay; 'twas to see Lady Wray
in her raiment, for I wish'd to be thusly attired.
White samite wore she, mystic, wonderful –
To her thews it did cling, like wet leaves.

383 **wholly:** entirely

384 **baptismal font:** in Christian churches, a basin of water for the symbolic washing away of sins

Yea, I did weep, 'til it struck like a thunderbolt –
I, too, could be beautiful, if I but believed.
Let us now give ourselves wholly to pleasure
in this baptismal font wherein
we may take dalliance far beyond measure
and wash ourselves of fear of sin.
Nightmares and daydreams alike shall we treasure.
Heigh-ho! These riches and more
do for us lie in store. Can'st thou see't?
Heigh-ho!

GENTLEMAN
We see much more besides!

FRANK
To dream, or to be? There is no question!

FRANK dives into the Basin and swims.

FRANK [*Sings.*]
Take thou those threads of thy dream and desire,
weave them to wakening, richly attired!

COLUMBIA, ROCKY, BRAD and JANET prepare to enter Basin.

ALL [*Sing.*]
Take thou those threads of thy dream and desire,
weave them to wakening, richly attired!

COLUMBIA, ROCKY, BRAD and JANET dive
into the Basin and swim.
FRANK directs Staff at EVERETT,
who regains movement and dances in his wheeled chair.

385 **crave nought but folly and squalor:** want nothing but foolishness and lazy living

386 **Saint Cyr:** a popular child saint with a strong following in France.
(For those who find Janet's statement at this point in *Rocky Horror* a bit confusing, Lili St. Cyr was a popular burlesque stripteaser of the 1940s and 1950s.)

387 **Awop-bop-a-loo-mop alop bam boom:** A seldom-used string of nonsense syllables common to English folk-songs... Okay, I'll cut you a break. When Tim Curry auditioned for the role of Frank 'N' Furter, he sang "Tutti Frutti".

388 **barb:** sting

389 **ply:** wield; use

390 **awry:** out-of-balance

391 **tabor's reply:** the beats of the drum. The pipe and tabor were a popular combination of instruments, and convenient, as they could be played together by a single skilled musician.

Pipe & Tabor.

EVERETT [*Sings.*]
>   *Fie! Heavens defend us! This is a trap!*
>   *Our wills grow weak, bound by his jewl'd collar!*
>   *To reason I must cling, like the spider to its string,*
>   *lest my mind like a worn thread do snap*
>   *and, maddened thus, I crave nought but folly and squalor.*

GENTLEMAN
Yea, folly and squalor!

BRAD [*Sings.*]
>   *This evening is a nightmare from which I cannot wake.*
>   *Like a babe who cries for Mother, I beg of thee to take*
>   *this dream away.*

JANET [*Sings.*]
>   *By Saint Cyr, whose good name be bless't,*
>   *I've a wish to come quite undress't!*
>   *My skin, lily-white,*
>   *would be a heavenly sight...*
>   *But it would unleash some civic unrest.*

GROUNDLING
Damn! I'd have paid extra to see that.

GENTLEWOMAN
Pray, Lord Frank, sing again!

FRANK [*Sings.*]
>   *Awop-bop-a-loo-mop alop bam boom*
>   *A thing wild and untamèd am I.*
>   *The venom'd bee's barb I do ply.*
>   *One ping of my sting sets your humors awry.*
>   *Your heart will out-skip the tabor's reply.*
>   *Cry Huzzah! and let slip the party hounds.*
>   *We'll dance 'til we drop whilst the music sounds.*

392 **tenure:** time of being in charge

393 **arcane:** mysterious; secret

Like spectacles of rosy glass,
let me see only that pleaseth me.

ALL [*Sing.*]
Things wild and untamèd are we.
We ply the venom'd barb of the bee.
One ping of our sting, out of humor you'll be.
Your heart will out-leap the pipe's highest key.
Fiddle-dee-dee! 'Tis fit for a spree!
Cry Huzzah! and let slip the party hounds.
We'll dance 'til we drop whilst the music sounds.
Like spectacles of rosy glass,
let me see only that pleaseth me.

[*All Dance.*]

Things wild and untamèd are we.
We ply the venom'd barb of the bee.
One ping of our sting, out of humor you'll be.
Your heart will out-leap the pipe's highest key.
Fiddle-dee-dee! 'Tis fit for a spree!
Cry Huzzah! and let slip the party hounds.
We'll dance 'til we drop whilst the music sounds.
Like spectacles of rosy glass,
let me see only that pleaseth me.

> *Enter RIFF-RAFF and MAGENTA,*
> *bedecked in otherworldly Attire,*
> *and with hair set all askew.*

RIFF-RAFF [*Sings.*]
Lord Frank N. Furter, the curtain falls
upon your tenure within these walls.
The arcane magic you have wrought
hath come to nothing, nil, and nought.

394 **repair:** return

395 ***Prima Noctae:*** Latin for "First Night"; the "right" of a lord to have sex with any common woman within his lands on her wedding night.

396 **stay me:** hold me back

397 **impel:** compel; force

398 **cleave:** cling

Your servant no more, I now command,
and imprison you, by law of our land.
Magenta, do the charm prepare.
To Transylvania we'll soon repair.

GENTLEMAN
Your servant no more, I now demand
Prima Noctae, by law of our land!

FRANK
Prithee, sir – forbear!
I can explain all!

RIFF-RAFF
Very well.
We have time for one more song.

FRANK [*Sings.*]
When I from our home world did take leave,
and kick'd its purple dust from off my soles...

ALL [*Sing.*]
...Fare thee well...

FRANK
...Was all I did say, and so I believ'd,
for none could stay me from my goals.

ALL
Now my soul doth impel...

FRANK
... me to turn 'round and to my home world cleave,
ne'er to go again; I've flipp'd my poles.

399 **din:** noise; racket

400 **surfeit:** overabundance

401 **mean chance:** misfortune

402 **Orpheus:** in Greek mythology, a gifted musician whose singing and lyre-playing could make stones weep. Upon the death of his wife Eurydice, his music took an unbearably mournful turn.

ALL
> *O down-derry-dell...*

FRANK
> *O pray, without guile, do assure me with a smile*
> *that this good news is true.*
> *for through tear-filled eyes I hath seen skies*
> *that are not green, but blue.*
> *and now I do know that to home I go.*

ALL
> *Now I do know that to home I go.*

FRANK
> *A meaningless din my existence hath been –*
> *I see it now, 'tis true –*
> *a surfeit of mean chance, sorrow and pain*
> *and designs I now do rue.*
> *But through tear-filled eyes I hath seen skies*
> *that are not green, but blue.*
> *And now I do know that to home I go.*

FRANK and ALL [*Sing.*]
> *Now I do know that to home I go.*
> *Now I do know that to home I go.*
> *Now I do know that to home I go.*

MAGENTA
Faustus, your sentimental lay
out-sighs even Orpheus.

RIFF-RAFF
Nonetheless, you presume too much.
I did say that we were to return to Transylvania,
but I meant only Magenta and myself.
I regret that you found my words misleading.

403 **a pale shade:** a ghost or spirit

404 **Two stars ... in one sphere:** The ancient Greek philosopher
Aristotle (384-322 BCE) proposed that the Universe was made of
"nested spheres", with Earth at the center. Each object that
appeared to cross the sky was attached to its own sphere; the
stars were all on the outermost sphere. In the Middle Ages, the
Jewish philosopher Maimonides (1135-1204 CE) wrote that
astronomers had discovered that the stars are at varying
distances from us, and that there appeared to be evidence that
Earth did not in fact stand at the center of the Universe. He
proposed in his *Guide for the Perplexed* that each star might have
its own sphere – but also that the entire idea of "nested spheres"
may in time be proven incorrect – no offense to the great
Aristotle.

405 **brook:** contain; support

406 **O celestial firmament!:** Good Heavens!

407 **grimoires:** books of magic spells

408 **ember:** spark from a fire

409 **massy:** massive

410 **smite:** strike with deadly force

411 **corpus:** body

You, Doctor Faustus Frank N. Furter,
are to remain here, as a pale shade,
perhaps, or a dim memory.
Two stars keep not their motion in one sphere;
nor can this castle brook two lords –
Knowest you that.

GROUNDLING
'Scuse me while I just whip this out...

RIFF-RAFF draws a Wand from his garment.

EVERETT
O celestial firmament! I hath seen
such an instrument in my grimoires.
'Tis a weapon of unspeakable power.

RIFF-RAFF
Aye, Doctor Everett. Knowest how
the wind that passes through a man's lips
can raise a dying ember to flame,
or blow it to ashes?
Behold, the Jovian bolt!
The very principle that, this evening,
did issue the breath of life into the dead clay
Of Rocky's massy form. Yet, in the space
of an eye-blink, it can smite a man
with lightning, tearing the very threads
of his corpus apart like so much cobweb,
leaving not even a body to mourn over.

GENTLEMAN
Ask a fool's question, Brad!

412 **oblivion:** nothingness. *Finito.* It's all over.

BRAD
Mean you to kill him? Prithee,
what is his crime?

EVERETT
You saw, Lord Brad, what became of poor Edward.
Society must needs be protected from such
as do murder their friends in cold blood
and serve them up at table.

GENTLEWOMAN
And pair them with white wine. Forsooth!

RIFF-RAFF
Verily, Doctor Everett. And now,
Doctor Faustus Frank N. Furter,
'tis your time. Bid *adieu* to this, all this,
your cell, your castle, your friends, this world
and the one from whence you came –
Bid adieu to it all, and to oblivion set thy sail.

GROUNDLING
Say bye-bye!

COLUMBIA screams. RIFF-RAFF sets his Wand against her.

COLUMBIA
O spite! O Hell! Riff-Raff, wherefore didst thou
blast me so? I did perhaps love not wisely,
but too well. Am I, therefore, to die
for so small offense?
[*Dies.*]

GROUNDLING
Yep.

413 **stalwart:** brave and bold

414 **the wheeling kites:** carrion-birds that often circle in the air above a battlefield, awaiting their yummy feast.

415 **imminence:** coming soon

FRANK makes to flee. RIFF-RAFF sets his Wand against him.

RIFF-RAFF
You see now, O Faustus, how perish those
who taste of Jove's fire!
Blood alight, all senses aflame,
no hero stalwart, of upthrust chin – Nay!
Only a trembling, fear-filled pup,
begging for death to bring end to his sorrow and pain.

FRANK receives a grievous wound and falls.

FRANK
O! I am slain! My body is wracked with pain.

ROCKY lifts FRANK upon his shoulders
and makes to climb the Tower.
RIFF-RAFF sets his Wand against ROCKY.

RIFF-RAFF
How now, O ape?
Loping upward the tower as a tree,
weighted down by your dying master?
Where canst thou go?
The wheeling kites know better than thee
the imminence of thy doom.
O shivering shocks!

The Tower falls,
casting ROCKY and FRANK into the Basin.

ROCKY
Now am I dead.
Now am I fled.

416 **incapable:** unaware

417 **insensate:** unable to feel anything

418 **fathoms:** A fathom is 1.8288 meters, or six feet. A little longer than two ells.

419 **beshrew my heart:** a mild expletive, roughly translated as "to curse". Rather like saying, "Well, I'll be damned."

My soul, if such a being as I hath soul,
is in the sky.
[*Dies.*]

FRANK
Poor Rocky, incapable of his own distress.
But not so I. I do but float awhile,
feeling my world grow ever colder,
colder, then to insensate.
My garment fabulous doth drink of this water,
and when, at last, a-heavy with drink it grows,
it will draw me down, some two ells depth.
Yet my soul will downward continue,
and some certain fathoms into darkness go.
[*Dies.*]

                                    GENTLEMAN
        This passion would go near to make a man look sad.

                                    GROUNDLING
        Does anyone have a handkerchief? [*Sniffles.*]

                                    GENTLEWOMAN
            Beshrew my heart, but I pity the man.

JANET
O grief! You killed them!

MAGENTA
Riff-Raff, dear brother, thought I
that you did love them. They lovèd you.

RIFF-RAFF
Nay! They liked me not.
He – Doctor Faustus – he never
held me in favor!

420 **Erebus:** in Greek mythology, one of the primordial gods, the first five beings formed from the void Chaos. Erebus was the personification of deep darkness and shadows.

421 **importune:** bad-mannered; impolite

422 **quit:** leave

423 **æther:** the upper atmosphere, as imagined by learned men of the time. It had been long known that air became thin and difficult to breathe as one climbed a mountain.

424 **slip:** escape

425 **transits:** orbits

426 **archipelago:** chain of islands. The term "galaxy", or even the concept of a galaxy as we know it today, did not yet exist.

The motions of his spirit were dull as night,
and his affections dark as Erebus.

EVERETT
Thou didst aright.

RIFF-RAFF
A decision had to be made.

EVERETT
And a sound decision it were.
I respect you for carrying it out,
though it meant dealing death.

RIFF-RAFF
Doctor Everett, I had not the opportunity
to offer condolences on the death
of young Edward Cutlet, your nephew.

EVERETT
Ah, alas, poor Edward.
Yes, well... An ungovernable child was he.
Perhaps 'twas all for the best.

RIFF-RAFF
It may seem importune to hurry a guest,
Doctor Everett; but you should quit this place
forthwith, whilst the possibility to do so
exists. My sister Magenta and I hath prepared
a charm by which this castle, each brick and pediment,
will rise bodily through the æther, like so much mist,
and slip this tiny globe. It will ascend the heights,
and move where stars do dance.
We will return to our world, a sphere named Transsexual,
that transits a star in the archipelago of Transylvania.

427 **portcullis:** a castle's protective gate

A Portcullis.

428 **undertaking:** mission; assignment

429 **cavort:** play and dance cheerfully

430 **dark refrains:** spooky repeated lyrics

431 **trip:** step

To this distant planet we shall return.
As for you, and your fellow human creatures,
go... now.

                              GENTLEMAN
                 Take care that the portcullis
                 strike thee not on the way out!

         Exeunt EVERETT, BRAD and JANET.

RIFF-RAFF
Our undertaking is completed, my most
beauteous sister, this matter drawn to close.
Soon shall we come unto the purple sands
of our beloved planet, to cavort 'neath its moons.

MAGENTA
Ah – Sweet Transsexual, land of night,
to make song, and turn a merry courant once more
to thy dark refrains. To trip lightly to one's right...

RIFF-RAFF
Thy pelvis move in attitude rude...

CHOIR [*Singing, from without*]
         That seize the brain besides the heart!
MAGENTA
On our world, prithee, the frolic begin!
Time's Warp and Weft we weave again!

RIFF-RAFF
Let us now touch elbows thrice, in the manner of our land,
for our victory we now hold most firmly in hand.

                              GROUNDLING
                 ... Among other things!

432 **e'en:** evening

433 **note:** notice

Exeunt RIFF-RAFF and MAGENTA.
Close curtain. Enter BRAD, JANET and EVERETT.
A peal of Thunder as the Image
of FRANK'S Castle is drawn into the Heavens.

EVERETT
For there is more in Earth and sky
than is dreamt in our Philosophy;
and this close encounter shown
to us that we are not alone.
Celestial beings this e'en we met –
and now we're bare and dripping wet.
This darkened wood doth chill my soul,
so let us to my mansion roll.

Enter THE BARD, bearing a Globe. Exeunt BRAD, JANET and
EVERETT.

THE BARD
We are but insects, you and I,
scraping for life until we die.
Upon the broad Earth's face we crawl,
which takes no note of us at all.
Through sky unmeasur'd it doth roll,
dust-mote in a vast cathedral.
So are we less than dust, and lost...

GENTLEMAN, GENTLEWOMAN
and GROUNDLING
Like your neck!

THE BARD
... in time, and space, and meaning...

CHOIR [*Singing, from without*]
Meaning...

434 **ebon:** black, like ebony

THE BARD places Globe on the stage.
Exit THE BARD.
Enter a SINGER, painted full of lips.

SINGER [*Sings.*]
    Philosophy and Fable, both alike in virtue...
    Two plays for the price of one.
    Doctor Faustus did his Creation build,
    only to lose him; and all were killed.
    Darkness hath folded its ebon wings
    over Brad and Janet's underthings.
    The servants and castle skyward soar'd,
    and left our world for distant shores.
    Fa la la la la...
    At the nighttime revels I tell thee of,
    two plays for the price of one.
    I would fain also go,
    Hey, nonny-nonny go ho...
    to the nighttime revels I tell thee of.
    By by, lully, lullay.

Exit SINGER.

EPILOGUE.

GENTLEMAN
Common Groundling, we hath found,
as it would seem, some common ground
'twixt us, here tonight –
Making with our sport two shows of one.

GROUNDLING
Yeah, whatever. Great show, aye?

GENTLEMAN
Verily. Dear wife, what think'st thou?

GENTLEWOMAN
In troth, I did come to enjoy it.
Should there another performance be,
I should take care to attire myself
more to the spirit of the occasion.

GENTLEMAN
You do my heart delight, milady!
As it happens, this show do play
each week at this time. We may
attend as oft as thou like.

GROUNDLING
Great! Hey, maybe we'll bump into each
other again at this.

435 **toss-pots:** pompous asses

GENTLEMAN
If we do meet again, why, we shall smile.

GENTLEWOMAN
… And weave Time's Warp and Weft
most merrily!

GENTLEMAN
And so I bid thee adieu.
Anon, then.

> *Exeunt GENTLEMAN and GENTLEWOMAN.*

GROUNDLING
Buh-bye!
Toss-pots! – These plays would be better
If they didn't all talk so funny…

> *Exit GROUNDLING.*

THE END

AFTERWORD

It was with considerable surprise that I discovered, sometime in the summer of 2018, that there was no Shakespeare-style spoof of *Rocky Horror Picture Show* on the market. The idea had come to me (I don't recall what prompted it), it seemed like a hoot, and I looked online to see if it had been done. There are a number of Shakespearean spoofs, of course – Adam Bertocci's *Two Gentlemen of Lebowski*, every single *Star Wars* movie, even *Hamlet* translated into the original Klingon tongue (inspired by a hilarious line in *Star Trek IV: The Undiscovered Country*, which featured Christopher Plummer as a Shakespeare-quoting Klingon) – but no *Rocky Horror*.

I could not believe my good fortune. I would have to remedy this situation.

*   *   *

As you no doubt already know, *Rocky Horror Picture Show* began as a rock opera (*The Rocky Horror Show*) by Richard O'Brien in the early 1970s and was made into a movie in 1975. It was intended from the get-go as a campy send-up of the cross-dressing scene and B-grade horror and sci-fi movies. The movie tapped into the subconscious of the teenage mind and assumed immediate cult status. It stands as a celebration of the exuberance and sexual experimentation that have always been, and will always be, part of the teen scene. Each year, new high school students are inducted into the ranks, usually by way of a midnight showing at some remote cinema at the behest of a mutual friend who has already been initiated. I find it quite comforting to see that its popularity remains strong!

Although *Rocky Horror* fans are legion, I am not exactly one of them. My musical tastes run very much toward the classical; and although I have a good time seeing the movie with family and friends, I didn't find it terribly compelling. My brother Stefan was our first initiate, and he brought the rest of us out to a cinema in the middle of nowhere, New Jersey so we could lose our virginity as well. He would rent it on videotape from time to time. Dad enjoyed watching us all dancing "The Time Warp" in the living room so much that he made it part of the reception at every wedding we've had or been invited to ever since. And I enjoy getting out on the floor and busting a move – up to and including reeling to the ground at the end – and fully intend to Time Warp at every single wedding in my future, for my own pleasure as much as to honor Dad.

*   *   *

Initially, I conceived of this as a fun little project to work on while taking breaks from an extremely tedious chore that had to be done – going through old paperwork and scanning anything I wanted to keep. I'd recycle boxes of old papers each week, and it was good to be rid of the clutter. But the task (of sorting, scanning, and recycling) was so very dull and repetitive that I needed something to help stave off the boredom of it all. Something to help me stay sane inside insanity, as it were. I had several big projects in the works, but I feared that if I got started on any of *those,* the mental investment required would preclude my ever getting this scanning/recycling thing done. I needed something fairly simple. Then (I think) a friend of mine made a passing reference to *Rocky Horror* on FaceBook, and something inside me clicked on. *Rocky Horror* seemed perfect: the story and script already exist; I only needed to retell it in a manner like unto the Bard.

This is a good deal more than just thee-ing and thou-ing everything, of course. (In fact, thees and thous appear only in dialogue between lovers, close friends and family. In business deals, formal settings or talk between people of differing social classes, our present-day pronouns are used. And when addressing a noble, titles are used, such as milord or Your Highness. This will be on Friday's quiz.) Fortunately, I grew up reading Shakespeare, so while I'm not really an expert, I don't have a problem with the language at all.

* * *

Since *Rocky Horror* has a "second script" consisting of audience participation, I decided to include it. During the show, I place the three specified audience members' lines against the right-hand margin, to make it easier to follow. Taking a cue from Shakespeare's own *The Taming of the Shrew*, which opens with a noble couple sitting down to attend a play given by amateurs, I added an Introduction (which the Bard called an Induction; that's not a typo) in which we're introduced to two audience members, who are joined by a third after the play starts; they also get an Epilogue together. It occurred to me that the hysterically silly play-within-the-play of Pyramus and Thisbe in *A Midsummer Night's Dream*, where the audience provides a running commentary, is very much the same thing. It seems that audiences at the Globe Theater did not always sit quietly with their hands folded in their laps. To the contrary – they sometimes gave the show the *Rocky Horror* treatment if they saw fit.

* * *

As all my "fairly simple" side-projects do, this turned out to be more involved than I'd anticipated. I immediately discovered that the songs were much more difficult to render than the dialogue. I tried whenever possible to match the meter of the original songs, but this could be a maddening challenge when the song referenced things that simply did not exist in Shakespeare's time. Right at the start, Trixie (the girl who sold ice cream at the theater where the original *Rocky Horror Show* premiered, and who sang the opening and closing songs) sings of a "Science-fiction double feature". In Shakespeare's time, study of the natural sciences was part of what was broadly termed "Philosophy" (and this is what Hamlet speaks of when he tells Horatio that "there is more in Heaven and Earth than is dreamt of in your philosophy"). The term "fiction" did exist, but its connotation seems to be closer to "deception" than "a story of something that didn't actually happen"; so "fable" seemed a better word to pair with "philosophy" to kludge together a stand-in for sci-fi. A fable is a fanciful story that nonetheless conveys a truth about ourselves, and the best science-fiction fits this description. As for the many B-movie references that fill out the song... they came out reading like a vague prophecy by Nostradamus! When "Philosophy and Fable" was done, I decided to continue with my project by focusing on the dialogue first and doing the songs afterward. This not only made the task less arduous, it helped determine some of the wording to the songs.

In the middle of "Time Warp", Columbia sings her solo. It begins, "I was walkin' down the street, just a-havin' a think, when..." So many, many songs begin this way, including English folk songs of past centuries. Someone sets out to take an outdoor stroll or ride, and meets someone, or at least eavesdrops on someone else's business. As I looked over Columbia's solo, and recalled her character's fate in the story – how she was a groupie of Frank's, then was rejected and cast aside – I remembered one particular folk song called "Early One Morning": a woman tells the entire sad tale of love found and lost at the hands of a brash lord who had tired of her. This is Columbia's story exactly, and so I decided – at the expense of the '50s-style riff – to have her sing to the tune of "Early One Morning". She reprises it later, in the song "Edward". I considered having her sing it briefly as she dies, but I think I gave her enough to say as she expires; I imagine in a production the musicians could play the tune once more while she talks herself to death.

*   *   *

As I went, I discovered several things I'd never noticed before. One was the basic plot to *Rocky Horror*, which had always sort of eluded me. The other was its close connection to Shakespeare's final play, *The Tempest*. (This same play was also the basis for the classic 1950's science-fiction film *Forbidden Planet*, by the way.) *The Tempest* even turns into a bit of a "floor show" in its final act. These revelations helped me to punch up the dialogue and make characters' motivations clearer. Also, in watching the movie again, I noticed that Brad wears a tartan cummerbund in the opening scene; therefore I portray him in Scottish attire in the illustrations to my version.

Since this whole business is a spoof of a musical that was itself a send-up of the tranny scene and '50s B-grade sci-fi and horror movies, I saw no harm in tossing in an occasional anachronism. The Groundling makes comments that at times make him seem more a product of the 20th Century. (Originally, I had considered making him a 20th Century man who can't figure out what happened to his favorite show, but that seemed a bit too much.) Shakespeare himself was not above using anachronisms, as evidenced by the chiming of a clock in *Julius Caesar* (set in a time when sundials were the most accurate timepieces available) and the delightful bit of wordplay "The iron tongue of midnight hath toll'd twelve" in *A Midsummer Night's Dream*, which is ostensibly set during the reign of Theseus, the hero who in Greek mythology slew the Minotaur in the labyrinth. Whether he was aware that they were out-of-place is a matter of speculation. Public education in Elizabethan England was actually quite thorough; the numerous mentions of Greco-Roman history and mythology throughout the Shakespeare plays would have been understood by his audience, whereas today we cannot make such an assumption and must explain these passing references in facing-page notes. However, as far as ancient times went, precious little was known outside of what was recorded in writing and the ancient ruins that still stood. Knowledge of the day-to-day life of a Greek or Roman citizen of ancient times was still a big gray area, as archaeology at the time was little more than sloppy tomb-robbing. Thus, in many cases, the characters, especially of the lower classes, are more reflective of English folk of the 16th Century than anyone else. Historical knowledge aside, it's more likely that audiences simply were not terribly concerned with verisimilitude. We still see this today; try watching some sweeping historical drama like *Braveheart* in the company of someone who actually *studied* up on Sir William Wallace, and you'll wonder how the film, so rife with inaccuracies, did so well at the box office (or why you chose to watch it with this nerd). The truth is, the facts don't matter so much to folks who just want to be entertained for a few hours. Therefore, I saw little harm in sneaking a few lines that hearken to literary works that post-date Shakespeare by decades or even centuries. The traditional tune of "Early One Morning" is from some time after Shakespeare's. I also slipped in a few bits from Samuel Taylor Coleridge, Alfred, Lord Tennyson, Charles Dickens, and even Gilbert and Sullivan – all 19th Century. Heck, I even shoehorned a line from Oscar Hammerstein and Jerome Kern's *Showboat* in there, which segues nicely into the next paragraph...

The theme of transvestitism not only rather dates *Rocky Horror* (I don't think most people are as shocked by it as they were in the early '70s), it poses a curious problem when doing a Shakespeare-style spoof as well. As you may very well know, acting in Shakespeare's day was strictly a man's job. Some directors would sneak their daughters into the cast from time to time – but this could never be publicized. It would have been scandalous in Elizabethan England. Therefore, audiences accepted that female roles were played by men in women's clothes. Dr. Frank N. Furter may scandalize our Gentlewoman by appearing in sexy ladies' undergarments; but the fact that he's *supposed* to be a man who dresses in women's clothing might have to be explained to her.

While Shakespeare takes care to give us the locale, and even specifies certain actions and props as needed, he never gives us much detail. The players would have to work out how they were going to convey the sense that we were now in a throne room, a battlefield, a blasted heath, a family mausoleum, or a marketplace. This was usually done through miming, although some costume changes could be done. There were, however, strict laws governing what one may wear, so if a man played a king, the best he was allowed to do was to wear his Sunday clothes and cap his head with a tin crown to indicate that he was the king. If he could actually afford gold brocade and ermine, he was too far above an actor's social station to be traipsing the boards in a public show. Sets were usually quite minimal. Fortunately, we are not so restricted nowadays, and can take a few liberties. I kept the stage direction and prop mention to a minimum, but I did give the layout of the set for Act II, Scene 3, and Act III. In the film, Act II, Scene 3 requires rapid transition between at least three sets, to the point of being awkward to stage – a problem best resolved with a two-level set representing the various locations. In Shakespeare's Globe Theatre, interestingly, this wasn't difficult at all. As you can see in the illustration I've provided, the building was three stories high, and the part of the second floor over the stage could be used as part of the set. (It is nearly certain that this is where Juliet's balcony was in *Romeo and Juliet*.) While Act III is all one set that breaks the fourth wall by including the theater, the cavorting in the giant basin is visually more interesting if the audience can see it, hence the mirror. Curtains were almost

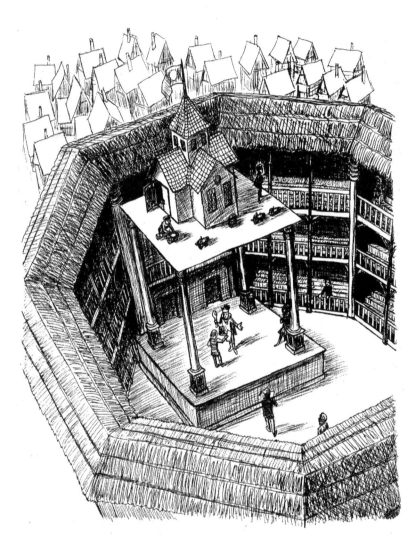

The Globe Theatre as it may have looked on the morning of 29 June, 1613.

never a part of Shakespeare's theater, but I include it here to allow for swift transitions to other locales and back again, or to allow for quick scene changes. For those who choose to stage this, I recommend building the castle sets as a single unit on wheels so it can be rotated. The cell can be converted to the dining-hall with ease by simply removing the cauldron and bringing in a table. I'm sure a professional set designer would know better than I how this would all work. As for the castle's ascent at the end, there was an upper platform called "The Heavens" for off-stage musicians to play in and sound-effects to be made. Had there been a need to hoist something aloft, it would have been drawn into The Heavens by means of thin ropes. On 29 June, 1613, the special effects crew set up some small stage cannons in The Heavens, to be fired during a triumphal scene in a play called *All is True*, which seems to have been a dry run for Shakespeare's *Henry VIII*, completed a few months later. Some wadding from a cannon landed on the theater's thatched roof, where it smoldered and started a fire. Within minutes the flames had spread throughout the octagonal roof, and a sloppy evacuation began. Nobody was killed, thankfully, but one man lost the use of his trousers when they caught fire. He doused the flames with a wooden can of ale. There was not enough ale to go around, however, and two hours later The Globe was a pile of charred timber.

* * *

I hope that you take as much delight in reading this as I did in writing it. Perhaps it will help some poor student who struggles to make sense of Shakespeare's flowery phrases, or inspire another to explore the Bard's canon beyond the few plays covered in high school. And perhaps it will enable *Rocky Horror* fans to enjoy their favorite cult classic on a whole new level.

Don't dream it – Be it.

To dream, or to be? There is no question!

The Globe Theatre as it may have looked on the morning of 30 June, 1613.

ABOUT THE AUTHOR/ILLUSTRATOR

Nicholas Dollak was born in 1967 in Long Branch, NJ. Since the age of three he knew that he wanted to be "an artist and a book-maker". At the time of this publication, he lives in Jersey City, NJ, creating art and writing whenever he gets the opportunity. You can see his artwork at https://ndollak.wordpress.com/

OTHER BOOKS
Written and illustrated by **Nicholas Dollak**

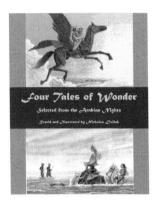

Jenna of Erdovon
http://amzn.com/1929084145

Four Tales of Wonder
https://amzn.com/B01GD6QTCW

Four Years and Change: An American Decameron

http://a.co/4uvVIq

Strikes and Gutters: The Rise, Fall and Papers, Business Papers of The Little Lebowski Shop
http://a.co/bwO

Printed in Great Britain
by Amazon

10528659R00153